The Secret of Willerby Grange

I0633671

Dorothy M. Mitchell

chipmunkapublishing
the mental health publisher

Dorothy M. Mitchell

Published by
Chipmunkapublishing
PO Box 6872
Brentwood
Essex CM13 1ZTUnited Kingdom

http://www.chipmunkapublishing.com

Copyright © Dorothy M. Mitchell 2011

Chipmunkapublishing gratefully acknowledge the support of Arts Council England.

Author Biography

Dorothy was born in a small village in Yorkshire just before the Second World War. She remembers ration books, her mum swapping coupons with other mums; one might need extra clothing coupons and another butter or meat coupons. Dorothy also remembers being in their garden air raid shelter as enemy bombs rained down over nearby towns and cities mostly at night; very frightening. Dorothy was only six years old, so memories are rather hazy. Her dad was in the Home Guard, or Dads' Army, as you may know it being called. She also thinks back to that time as being very hard. One memory she recalls vividly and that was sweet shops without any sweets! You could get sherbet and your weekly ration of sweets or chocolate; this added up to about two ounces a week. Not much by today's standards. Dorothy remembers the shelf where her mum kept the sweets, well out of reach of little fingers.

Dorothy moved to Evesham in 1954 with her mum and dad and her younger brother and sister. Her dad had a job as Steward of the local Working men's club.

She married a local lad when she was eighteen. Her first son Andrew was born when she was twenty-one, her second son David when Dorothy was twenty-seven.

Dorothy was diagnosed with Multiple Sclerosis at the age of thirty-seven. She has suffered many painful relapses and seen the inside of many hospitals.

She was widowed at the age of fifty-three. Her life at that time was at a low ebb.

Eighteen months after her husband died she was invited to go to the local Pentecostal Church. Her thought at the time was, why not? I can't feel any worse than I do right now. Well to cut a long story short, Dorothy met, at the church, the man who was to become her second husband. Ken had been widowed about a year before Dorothy.

That was almost eighteen years ago.

Dorothy found she had a flare for writing, and to her joy CHIPMUNKA publishers picked her up. She has much to thank them for; they have to date published two of her novels and are at the moment working on her third. Dorothy would like to thank her sons Andrew and David, and Ken her husband, for all their help and support. Dorothy would also like to thank her good friend and fellow writer Martin P Buckley for his help.

Dorothy says all these must have the patience of saints.

Ben Bristow is married to Jess. They have two children, Alice and Jack, and they live in a small village in the Cotswolds. Ben is left an inheritance by an uncle, a rambling old House called Willerby Grange, situated on the East Yorkshire coast. The house dates back to the year 1570 and is steeped in a chequered history. It is full of intrigue and mystery, strange noises and even stranger discoveries. This book will fascinate the reader from the first page to the last.   Read and enjoy.

Dorothy M. Mitchell

CHAPTER ONE
Leaving

"But dad, I don't want to live in Yorkshire! We belong here. Jack won't want to go either."

Ben Bristow looked at his daughter. "You don't know what you're saying, Alice. You'll love Yorkshire."

"But I won't, dad! I'm not going!" Alice stood petulant, arms crossed in front of her, that stubborn look on her face. She was ten years old, a young ten. "What about school? I've just been picked for the netball team. All my friends are here. It's not fair. Who wants to go to rotten Yorkshire? It's a dump."

"Now then, that's enough." Ben was fed up of listening to all the negative reasons why they shouldn't move north. Alice was used to getting her own way. He knew it was the fault of Jess and himself. They had indulged their children far too much. Alice had been a sickly child, born premature, in and out of hospital for the first three years of her life. This was where the spoiling started: Alice because she was poorly, Jack, because Ben and Jess felt they didn't want him to feel left out.

Jack was a quiet eight year old boy, who loved to read and play with Montgomery his dog, a soppy collie cross, given to him for his sixth birthday. Montgomery and Jack were almost inseparable. Jess came into the kitchen.

"I could hear all the commotion from upstairs," she said, and looked at Ben and Alice. Her husband and daughter were usually the best of friends, but since the proposed move to Yorkshire, Alice seemed to be blaming her dad for disrupting her life so much. To be honest, Jess herself wasn't feeling all that happy. Since Ben had been left that inheritance, life for them had been turned upside down.

A letter had arrived from a solicitor in East Yorkshire about two weeks before asking Ben to get in touch regarding the death of an old uncle, by the name of Reuben Bristow. It seemed that Reuben was an eccentric who never married and his brother James and he had fallen out many years ago and completely lost touch with each other.

James was Ben's father, and although Ben knew of a skeleton in the family cupboard he didn't know what it was, because his father would never speak of it. He had taken the secret to his grave. So Ben had grown up with the knowledge that something had caused his father a great deal of anguish. This was reflected often in the pain he could witness in the sad eyes of his dad.

Ben had loved his father, and although he would always have fond memories of growing up with a good mum and dad, there was just a blank. Something bad had happened in the family and he really needed to know about it.

Ben had been an only child, so when he and Jess met and married, it was wonderful that they had been blessed with two children, Alice and Jack. Oh how Ben wished he could fill his family with the same enthusiasm for the imminent move to Yorkshire as he himself felt.

It seemed to his mind that unanswered questions would somehow be put in place with this move to Yorkshire.

"How do you all feel about going to Yorkshire for the weekend?" Ben had asked his family.

He was eager to start a new life. The inheritance was more than his wildest dreams could have imagined and

Ben was eager to see Willerby Grange. So with eagerness he said to the family,

"Come on, you three, we're off to the seaside." Jess smiled. Was she ready for a new life away from everything? She knew the small village of Everby on the edge of the Cotswolds was the place she called home. She and Ben had both been brought up in the village, and she knew that Ben's family came into the area shortly after he was born, from the north somewhere. Although they'd grown up in the same village, she and Ben didn't meet until they were pupils at the local high school, living as they did at either end of Everby, and attending different primary schools.

Jess knew at the tender age of sixteen that she loved Ben Bristow, a quiet, rather shy boy, with the bluest eyes she had ever seen eyes that were gentle and soft, with a sadness that she couldn't define. His unruly blond hair didn't look as if it ever saw a comb and Ben seemed to seek her out as well. In fact, the feeling was mutual between them both, so it seemed natural for them to marry as soon as they could.
When Jess was eighteen and Ben twenty, they had tied the knot. The village church had been packed with well wishers. That seemed a long time ago and lots had happened in both of their lives over the years.

Ben's father had died years before, leaving many unanswered questions about what had always made him so sad. This in turn had always troubled Ben. Her own father had passed away just after Alice was born, so her mother had lived alone ever since. It had always been a comfort to Jess that her mum lived a few minutes away, so she could keep an eye on her. This was part of the reason for Jess feeling apprehensive about moving so far away.

"Come on Jess, You look miles away love, what is it?" said Ben.

"Oh, Ben, it's Mum. I can't leave her," Jess replied.

Ben saw the anxious look in the eyes of his beloved Jessica. He was aware of the turmoil going on in that pretty head. He was very fond of his mother-in-law. She was a good person, and he knew that she was very fond of them and the children adored their grandmother.

"Do you think she would like to come to Yorkshire with us?" said Ben, with a twinkle in his eye.

"Oh Ben, shall I ask her?" This was what Jess had been hoping for, as she planted a kiss firmly on the lips of her husband. "I love you," she whispered. Ben smiled.

Celia Marchent had been dreading the imminent move of her family to Yorkshire. It was such a long way. She would never have said what she thought, because she was a decent sort, but since Tom had died, she had become accustomed to knowing that Jessica, Ben, and the children were just around the corner, so to speak. So when the question was asked, she said she would love to move to Yorkshire with her daughter and family.

Her cottage held many fond memories of happier times, when Tom was alive and Jessica was growing up, but she had been given this chance, and it was time to move on; she was still young enough at sixty two to start another new life with the family who meant the world to her, so the cottage was put on the market. "We're off to Yorkshire for the weekend, to look over Willerby Grange," said Ben to his happy mother,"Would you like to come with us? Celia smiled at Ben, the man who had made her daughter so happy. This was the start of a new life for them all, and where would it lead? Celia had a feeling that they were all at the beginning of a wonderful adventure, and it all centred around Willerby Grange on the East Yorkshire coast

CHAPTER TWO
The Adventure Begins

The Bristow family decided to go to Willerby Grange, starting early Friday morning. "We can pick up the keys from Somers, Wilkins & Dobbs. They are the solicitors dealing with the legal stuff!" said an excited Ben to Jess. "Alice! Will you please get a move on? I asked you ages ago to take Hetty and Montgomery round to Mrs Walker's. She will think we aren't going"

"Oh, Dad, do we have to go to Yorkshire?"

"Yes we do, young lady. You never know, Alice! If you give it a chance, you may find this weekend very enjoyable."

"Oh, come on, Alice," said her brother Jack. "We are going to the seaside. Trust you to spoil everything! Gran, tell Alice to stop being a spoil sport."

Celia Marchent had just arrived. She was aware that young Alice was being difficult, and she also realised that because of her granddaughter's sickly start in life, Ben and Jess had spoilt her rather; so it wasn't all the fault of the girl. If she could, Celia would do all she could to remedy the situation.

"Come on, you two! I can hardly wait to see what our new home is like." She put a loving arm around each of her grandchildren. "When we get to Willerby Grange I'm going exploring. The pictures your dad showed us looked very exciting. The grounds look super. Orchards of fruit trees, and as soon as we get there I'm going to pick apples"

"And me Gran," said an excited Jack.

"Will there be any squirrels, Gran?" said Alice, who seemed to be making an effort."

"Oh, sure to be, darling, in such a lovely old place as Willerby Grange. Who knows what we will find? I can't wait to get there and start the adventure."

Jess gave her mum a knowing smile. Celia Marchent had always been able to get the best out of her grandchildren; a natural, patient and loving way worked every time. It had always been obvious to Jess that her mother adored her grandchildren. The bond between them was special. Jess gave her mum a hug. "I'm so pleased that you are coming with us," she said.

The Thursday before the trip Ben had phoned the solicitor's office to make arrangements for the keys to be ready when they arrived at Axenbey village the following morning.

So the car duly packed with everything but the kitchen sink was driven out of the drive at six thirty a.m. with shouts of, "We're off at last! Did you pack the hamper Mum?"

"Yes dear, and the sleeping bags, and a bucket and spade each," Jess answered a very excited Jack.

He had got over the idea of bringing Montgomery, with the promise that they would all be living at Willerby Grange soon and Montgomery would be happier with Mrs Walker for the time being as he wasn't a very good traveller. Ben had arranged with the vet to give each pet a pill on the morning of the big move, so this would help them both to travel in as much comfort as possible.

"When will we get there?" said Alice.

"Soon, love," said a very patient Celia. She was sat in the back of the car, a child each side of her. It was about two hours into the journey. When they had counted red cars, cows in fields, and tractors, they tried to count sheep, but there were just too many. They went through towns and villages, and countryside that could almost have been the Cotswolds.

"We're here!" said Ben, when he saw the notice: WELCOME TO AXENBEY. "We've arrived."
The first thing to take Jess's eye was the fact that it was market day. Ben had parked the car down a narrow street, which ran alongside a small tree-lined square. On the left hand corner was a mini market; next door to that was a bakery. The door to the shop was open, and she could see a couple of small tables covered in blue gingham cloths, and the smell of fresh roasted coffee teased her nostrils.
Around the square, stalls selling a variety of goods were setting up. There was an air of business. Across from the mini market was a launderette; next door was what looked like a betting shop, then an ice cream parlour. Opposite where the car was parked, on the wall of an old fashioned looking building, was the sign, 'Somers, Wilkins & Dobbs, Solicitors since 1809.'
"Well, would you believe our luck?" said Ben. "Why don't we all go into the café and have a bite to eat, then Celia, perhaps you would take the children to the market, while Jess and I go and have a word with the solicitors. I'm sure some of the stalls would interest you."
"Oh, yes please," said Jack. "Come on, Gran."
"That's a good idea," said Gran. "But first things first, let's go and enjoy a cup of that delicious-smelling coffee. You two will probably want a sticky bun and some pop."

When they had finished their refreshment, Ben and Jess went off to the solicitors, and Celia and the children set off to explore the market stalls after arranging to meet back at the car in an hour.

"Ah here you are; Mr and Mrs Bristow, we meet at last," said the solicitor. "Did you have a pleasant journey? My name is Julian Somers, senior partner in the business."

They talked at length about the will, and all that the move to Yorkshire and Willerby Grange would mean to the family. "You will love the old Grange! It's steeped in history, built in 1570, in the reign of Elizabeth I. Over centuries it must have seen many changes. How many, we will never know, but I do so wish you all the best in your good fortune."

With that Julian Somers handed over the keys to the Grange, having first given Ben and Jessica all the information they needed about schools for the children, amenities in the area, and so forth.

"Oh, Ben! I still can't believe it," said Jess.

"Well it's true, love. We are the proud owners of a beautiful old manor house. Come on sweetheart, let's go and find the others."

Julian Somers had given them the directions to the Grange so off they went. Celia and the children were waiting, arms full of carrier bags. "We've had a super time, Mum. The market was smashing. Gran bought us a torch each, and some sweets."

Jess smiled at her excited offspring. "Come on then. In the car the pair of you. We're off to Willerby Grange"

CHAPTER THREE
Willerby Grange

From the village of Axenby, the family travelled along the coast road for about two miles. The sun was shining and it was a lovely August day. There were a few cottages dotted about as they travelled along winding country lanes, past a few farms, with sheep and cows in the fields, mostly just standing about, doing nothing much.

"Do you think they get fed up, Gran?" asked Alice.

"I expect so, Alice, wouldn't you, if you were just stood in a field all day?"

"Oh, Gran, you are funny," Alice replied. She was glad her Gran was coming with them.

"I can see the sea! Look, Alice," said an excited Jack.

They all looked to where Jack was pointing. They had emerged from a tree-lined narrow road, and to the left was an expanse of sea, way down below them. To the right, however, was a narrow road that swept back from the edge of the cliff. Ben turned the car into the drive of Willerby Grange, and stopped outside two large wrought-iron gates, one slightly open.

He got out and went towards the gates. As he pushed on the one that was ajar, a voice said,

"Hang on, sir. I'm coming!" From the left hand side of the drive, an elderly man scurried from behind a group of trees. "I've been expecting you. Mr Somers rang me and said would I introduce myself. You must be Mr Benjamin Bristow and family. My name is Barnaby

Sykes." The old man ran a weather eye over the young gent before him.

"So you're Master Ben. Well I never! It's nice to meet you at last. Mr Reuben talked of you a great deal."

"Who's that man, Mum?" said a curious Jack. "He looks very old."

"I don't know, love. Dad will tell us shortly."

Whilst they waited Celia, Jess, and the children got out of the car. "This looks just like a park to me," said Celia to Jessica, as Alice and Jack took off down the drive. Jess and her mum stood and stared in awe.

From the large gates, a winding drive forked in two directions. To the left was a large group of trees, comprising willow, mighty oak, spruce, and many others that they were unable to put a name to.

The side of a building was just visible from where they were standing. "That must be part of the Grange, Jess," said Celia. There looked to be acres of well tended grass to the right.

As they looked down over the massive grounds they saw what looked like an old building, as big as a house, nestling beneath the trees

"I wonder what that is," said a very curious Jess. "It looks very old and rather comfortable." She made a note to investigate the building later.

All the trees were in full leaf. It was a magic place.

"Oh, Jess, did you see that squirrel?"

"Yes, Mum, and I can hear seagulls," said Jess.

Ben came to where Jess and Celia were standing.

"Meet our gardener, Mr Barnaby Sykes. We have been having a little chat. He lives in the old coach house over there. I'm very happy with what he's been telling me, and I will fill you both in later about what he's said."

Jess had received her answer; the building in question was the Coach House; how very interesting. And what's more, the old boy lived there!

Ben jumped into the car and set off down the drive. "We'll walk down," said Jess. "I want to explore the grounds. Come on, Mum."

Barnaby Sykes tipped his cap to the ladies. "If you carry on down and keep to your right, you will come to the house."

Ben set off, turned and disappeared from view. Celia and Jess followed.

"Mum, quick, come and see the mansion!" It was a very excited Alice.

"She's perked up," said Celia.

The ladies hurried around the corner then stopped. Jess gasped! Was this real? They were standing at the front of Willerby Grange.

"This is enormous! What a house!" said Celia.

There was a very large doorway supported by two ornate pillars and the door itself looked like solid oak. Three steps led up to it and a large clematis climbed its way up the two pillars, rather overgrown, but it formed a beautiful arch. It was intertwined with passion flowers, and old-fashioned roses. The scent was overpowering.

As you looked along the length of the Grange, Virginia creeper snaked its way between windows, climbing in some parts right up to the roof.

"Oh, Ben! This is such a beautiful house," exclaimed Jess, who was overcome. "I just can't believe that we will be living here soon."

"Well, sweetheart, get used to it, because in a few weeks we will be living in the Grange," said Ben as he placed a kiss on Jess's forehead; he loved her so much.

Yes, it was a truly wonderful place, and they all knew that they were in for the time of their lives. Answers to questions that had plagued his life for so long were going to be found here. Jess also felt a stirring in her heart; Yes, fate had mapped out that their destiny was here, a brand new life in Yorkshire.

Willerby Grange, Idle Wood was to be their new home in a few weeks.

"Come on! Let's go into the house," said a wide eyed Alice.

They went towards the large oak door, and Jack was first up the steps, followed by Alice.

Ben was eager to gain entry to his new home.

"Come on you two. Let the dog see the rabbit!"

Ben eased past the excited pair, walking gingerly on steps strewn with debris and dried twigs. He put the enormous key into the lock and the door swung open with a loud groaning creek.

"Come on, Jess. You first," said Ben, holding out his hand. Jess took hold, climbed the steps and walked into a future that was to be so amazing that as time went on it would become more and more evident that life in Yorkshire for this fortunate family was to contain more excitement than any of them could ever have imagined.

"Just look at the hall! It's massive!" said Alice standing, mouth wide open. "Mum, it's a palace!"

The family gazed in awe. Opposite the door was a wide staircase and an ornate balustrade went up each side of the stairs, and carried on to the right and left along the landing. The whole structure seemed to form a semi-circle with lots of doors leading into what the family presumed would be bedrooms.

On the ground floor to either side of the stairs the hall continued as far back as you could see. "Oh, Mum, have you ever seen such beautiful tiles in all your life?"

said Jess, who was bowled over with the beauty and feel of the lovely old house. The flooring in the hall was magnificent; red, green, and dark yellow tiles formed a lovely parquet effect.

"I wonder if they have been here since the Grange was built," said an equally enthralled Celia.

The children ran across the hall by the side of the central staircase and disappeared into the back of the house, with shouts of, "Look at this. Oh, I love it here!" Jess, Celia and Ben followed the happy sounds, to discover for themselves the joys of all Willerby Grange had to offer them in their new lives on the East Yorkshire coast.

"Where are they both?" said Ben and the ladies as they followed the voices of the children into the back of the house.

"Here we are," said Jack, with laughter in his voice. He was seated on an enormous faded blue settee in a large room. There were various items of furniture comprising two easy chairs like the faded blue of the settee. Against the far wall was a large, highly polished sideboard, situated between two very large windows draped in red velvet. The carpet had seen better days, this being a sort of grey blue in colour.

"This is in need of a woman's touch," said Ben. Celia, who was thinking along the same lines, thought how sad the room looked, but wouldn't it be beautiful when she and Jess got to work on the old place.

She walked over to one of the windows. The garden was lovely, as she looked out onto weeping willow and mighty oak trees set in a blaze of colour from a variety of well established bushes and flowers. It was easy to see that the garden was well tended by expert hands.

"Oh, Jess, I can hardly wait to get out there," said Ben, who had always liked to potter. Now if his work permitted, he was looking forward to enjoying the pleasure this beautiful garden offered him.

As a chartered accountant he never seemed able to find enough spare time, but now, since their good fortune had brought about such a change for them all, he was determined that they would each enjoy this new life. Willerby Grange was a gift he wasn't going to take for granted. He meant to grab hold of life with both hands and live it, and oh, how he wished he could tell his father of his good fortune. For Ben felt it would, in some way, start to heal the wounds that had been so evident in the lives of the Bristow family for so long.

The family continued to explore the beautiful house, and downstairs they counted five sitting rooms, most of them shabbily furnished. A horse hair sofa dominated one of the rooms. "This must have come out of the Ark!" said Ben.

"It's not very comfortable, either," said Alice, who had just come in from the garden. "Oh, I just love this place. Come on, let's carry on exploring."

With that every room was investigated. The one that most impressed Jess was the dining room. "Look at the walls, Ben. Have you ever seen anything like that?" she said.

The whole wall was covered from floor to ceiling in carved, ornate dark oak panels. In the centre of the room was a long dark wooden table surrounded by heavy wooden chairs with high backs. A sideboard stood in a bay window, which looked out onto the front garden. The room was overshadowed by two mature weeping willows, and a crystal chandelier hung in all its opulent splendour from the yellowing ceiling.

In the centre of the far wall was an enormous dark stone fireplace, so large it seemed to dominate the room. It stood higher than the average man. In the hearth was a large iron grate discoloured from frequent use. Smoke stains were on the front of the fireplace. "Isn't this a lovely room, Jess?" said Celia, who was having difficulty taking all this in.

"Oh, Mum! I can hardly wait to get started on our new home. I just know we are going to be happy here."

Ben looked towards Jess and Celia. He could almost hear their brains ticking over, for home making was a woman's

prerogative. Those two were going to be in their element as ladies of the manor. Ben sighed with contentment. They were in for some hard work, he knew that, but judging by the enthusiasm displayed by each member of the family, the following months, even years, would be a most enjoyable adventure.

"I wonder where that door leads to," said Jess to her mum, as they came into the kitchen. The door in question was old and pitted with ages of frequent use.

"I'll bet it's been there ever since the Grange was built," said Celia. She pulled open the door which revealed a dark narrow staircase leading steeply upwards. "I'm going up, are you coming Jess?"

With that, both ladies started to ascend the stairs very gingerly, as there weren't any rails, but the stairs being walled on either side meant they were able to steady the climb.

On reaching the top they found a small square landing. To the right was another door. "It's a bathroom. Just look at that old roll top bath," said Celia, "isn't it lovely?" Jess opened a door directly opposite. The ladies walked into a large room. To the left was a large window devoid of curtains. There were bits and pieces of furniture scattered about the room, most in need of repair.

"This must have been used as a store room for a long time, judging by the age of most of the stuff." Celia nodded in agreement, "And doesn't it smell musty?" Opposite the window was another door. Jess opened it. Both stood in amazement, for they were looking at a long landing, going to the right and left. And yet another staircase that appeared to lead to the main house. "I'll bet this was the maid's quarters," Jess said to her mum, "that's why it leads from the kitchen." Celia nodded. "It must have been hard work in those days."

"There you are," said Ben. "I thought you pair had got lost."

"Oh Ben, you should just see it up there, another bedroom, and bathroom."

"My goodness, we will be able to have a bath each" said Ben with a smile.

The family carried on exploring the Grange. The children ran from room to room, with shouts of "Wow, look at this," as yet another point of interest was discovered. An excited Alice ran to her dad. "Oh, when can we move here?"

"Soon," said her dad. "But there is much to do before we finally leave Everbey, so I suggest we enjoy this weekend, take a good look around the area, find a shop where we can buy some bread and milk and a local newspaper, and I suppose you two would like a sticky bun?" "Yes, please" said Jack, "I'm a bit hungry."

So with that, the family piled into the car. "Did you lock the door Ben?" said Celia. "Yes I did. Now come on, it's mid afternoon already. Let's go and have high tea at the seaside".

So leaving the Grange, they set off to explore what was soon going to be their new home. They drove along the coast road until they were in Axenbey. "Ben, stop here, that looks like a nice place. Shall we have a cup of tea before we do anything else?"

"Good idea," said Ben. So the family walked over to the restaurant, sat down, and took in the atmosphere.

"Can I help you sir?" said a kind looking waiter.

"Three teas please, a selection of cakes and a bottle of pop for these two" said Ben, smiling up at the waiter.

"Certainly sir."

"Isn't this a nice place?" said Jack, tucking into a very jammy doughnut.

"It's lovely darling, and can you see the beach over there? I think Montgomery will love it as well," said his mum.

The family sat for a while, enjoying the feel of this pretty restaurant.

"Can I get you anything else sir?" It was the nice waiter.

"No thanks," said Ben, "that was a lovely cup of tea."

The waiter, thinking to himself what a nice gent, continued to converse with Ben.

"No doubt we will come here again." "Are you on holiday sir?"

"Just a long weekend at the moment" Ben told him. "But we will very shortly be coming to live near Axenbey, just along the coast in fact. About two miles from here, a place called Idlewood. Do you know it?"

"Yes. I know Idlewood," said the waiter. "It's a beautiful spot; very rugged, but not much there though sir, except for the Old Grange. A recluse lived there for many years. Passed away not long ago. Left everything in the house just as it was. I am a friend of the gardener, that's how I know about the Grange."

Jack, mouth full of cream bun, interrupted the conversation. "It's our house now, we're coming to live there soon"

"My! So you must be Mr Bristow and family? Well, I never! It's a small world and no mistake. You'll have met Barnaby Sykes then. He's lived in the old Coach House for years, and his missus used to look after the old boy."

Ben could hardly take this news in, and Jess and Celia were likewise incredulous, and both sat dumbstruck. "If you were to tell anyone that this had happened to you they wouldn't believe it. I knew we were in for the adventure of our lives," said Celia to Ben and Jess, "but this is almost unbelievable."

Ben shook hands with the waiter. "I'll bet you could tell us something of the history of Willerby Grange," he said.

"I could that," the waiter replied, "but I know someone who could tell you a lot more. Why don't you all come in for your Saturday lunch tomorrow? I will introduce you to a man who can give you all the information you require."

Ben thanked the waiter for all his help and, with a promise to be back at the restaurant at one o'clock the next day, the family left to do a short tour of Axenbey before returning to Willerby Grange.

The ride back was a bit strange, for in a short time they had learned more about their new home from a complete stranger, albeit a nice stranger, than any of them had ever expected.

"I knew this move was going to be more exciting than any of us could have imagined," said Celia, " I liked the waiter. I feel we were meant to go to that particular restaurant, and that he's all part and parcel of the whole affair. As I've said on a number of occasions, it's all been mapped out for us."

After the walk round Axenbey, finding their bearings and buying the goods required, the family were back in the car, on their way back to the Grange. By now it was almost dusk as they travelled along the coast road. The tide was out and the beach below looked almost deserted. A lone seagull circled above them, calling his plaintive cry.

"I wonder why seagulls sound so melancholy," said Jess, who was an animal lover. "I don't know, love," said Ben. "To me their sound just means we are at the coast, and we'll be hearing plenty more of them once we move to Willerby Grange. After all, our full address will be: Willerby Grange, Gulls Cry, and Idlewood East Yorkshire."

"I think it's a lovely address," said Alice from the back of the car. The car carried on for a little while, then came to a stop.

"Here we are, pile out," said Ben.

Once they were inside the house it was decided to sort out the sleeping bags before it got too dark, for although the Grange had been left to Ben, including its furniture, the adults rightly thought that the beds would be damp.

"Anyway, it will be more of an adventure," said Celia to her grandchildren. "Come on, you two."

With that, Alice and Jack followed their grandmother, armed with a sleeping bag each. "Don't forget the torches, darlings," said Celia, who was in her element. "It will be dark soon because the electricity has been turned off. Your dad is lighting a fire in one of the sitting rooms, so won't that be cosy? We can all have a hot drink once the fire gets going."

"This old copper kettle will be just the job," said Ben as he placed the heavy pot in the centre of the flames. "And the old Belling sink came in useful to keep the milk and butter cool."

"Can we all sleep in here?" asked Jack.

"Why Jack, are you scared?" said Alice.

"I am," said Celia, sensing that Jack didn't want to sleep alone in this strange old house.

"Why don't the three of us sleep in here?" said Celia to the children.

"That's a splendid idea," said Ben. "Jess and I will choose a bedroom upstairs."

"Isn't this exciting?" said Jack. "Come on then, Gran. Let's get settled."

With that Jess and Ben took a sleeping bag each and after "Good night, sleep tight," all round, they all tried to do just that, but it was so difficult. The old Grange had noises of her own: creaking, sighing sounds could be heard.

"Is the old girl welcoming us? Happy that she wouldn't be alone any more?" These were the thoughts that played on Celia's mind as she drifted into a peaceful sleep. She was going to love The Grange.

"Come on, you lot. It's Saturday morning and time you were all out of bed." It was Ben. Jess was awakened by the smell of fried bacon, and Celia and the children were also ready for a taste of that delicious breakfast.

Ben had the fire going in the enormous fireplace.

"You were all fast asleep when I came in, hope you didn't mind, Celia?"

Celia smiled. "No, of course not; it's all part of the adventure," she replied.

As they were tucking into bacon sandwiches, there was a knock at the door. It was the gardener.

"Oh, come in, Mr Sykes," said Ben.

"Call me Barnaby," said the old chap. "I meant to show you something yesterday, regarding how you can keep your milk cool. Come with me, Ben." The rest, intrigued as to what the old man had to say, followed him outside.

"You see that piece of slate down on the ground?" said Barnaby.

Ben looked puzzled, and said yes.

Turning to Jack, the old boy said, "Lift it up."

Jack did as he was asked and the removal of the slate revealed the top of a drainpipe, the perimeter of which was about eight inches round. Barnaby continued.

"My father sunk that pipe many years ago. Long before the Grange ever saw a fridge. It will keep your milk and butter as cold as a frosty Christmas."

"How wonderful," said Jess. "Your dad was very clever. Thank you, Barnaby. That will be most helpful until we get a fridge when we move to the Grange in a few weeks' time. Thanks again, Barnaby."

"Pleased to be of assistance sir," Barnaby replied.

"I'd like a chat before we go back to Everby," said Ben to this very likeable man.

With that the gardener put up his hand and walked away in the direction of the Coach House.

Celia addressed the children "It's 9:30; how do you two fancy going down to the beach? We might as well whilst we're here"

"That would be smashing, Gran. Shall we take a ball?" said Jack, who was all for it.

"Yes, if you like, love. We'll take towels just in case you both feel like a dip." So with that Celia, Alice and Jack set off for the beach.

They had discovered a gate the day before when investigating the orchard. On opening it they discovered a sloping path, quite narrow, with coarse bracken growing along either side.

"My, this hasn't been used in ages, so be careful you two," said Celia rather warily. "The path is a bit steep!"

Jack was bounding along, not a care in the world. "Gran, isn't this lovely?"

Alice took Celia's hand, and whispered, "I know I didn't want to come to this place but I just love it, and I'm sorry I was such a pain."

"That's all right, love. I was unsure myself, but I feel just like you, and I can't wait to move in here."

Great fun was had on the beach, in and out of the sea, playing with the giant ball. Celia looked at her wristwatch – 11:15 am.

"We'd better be getting back. We have to be in Axenby at 1pm. Come on, let's pack up and make our way back to the Grange."

When they arrived home Jess asked if they'd had a nice time down on the beach. "Mum, it was lovely. There was no-one else there but us."

"Is it our own private beach?" said Jack.

"Not sure dear, perhaps Dad knows," said Jess.

On being asked the question;"I think so," said Ben. "I must study the deeds."

"Go and have a wash and comb your hair. It's almost time to set off. You'd better visit the bathroom, Jack;" said his mother. "Then when we're all ready, it's into the car, and let's get off to Axenby."

They went to their special restaurant again. It was quite busy. "Nice to see you all again," said the kindly waiter, whom they met the day before. "Come along in."

They were shown to a table by one of the windows.

"Dad, look at all the boats out on the sea," said a very excited Jack.

"Yes," said the waiter, "you are fortunate. It's the tall ships race. They're just leaving the harbour. It's always a fine spectacle." With that, the waiter gave Ben a menu. "I'll be back in a few minutes," he said. "The gentleman you have come to see will be here shortly. He usually arrives around I pm every Saturday and Sunday, but speak of the devil.

"Afternoon, Mr Garside" said the waiter. "Nice to see you again. There are some people here who would like to meet you. They are the new owners of Willerby Grange, and I mentioned you to them yesterday."

Alex Garside smiled at the strangers.

"How can I help you?" he said, shaking hands with the family.

Well," said Ben, "We were here yesterday, and we were asking the waiter if he could give us any information on the Grange. He said he could tell us a little, but he knew a man who could tell us all we wanted to know. I presume you are the man in question."

"Mr Bristow, how very fascinating," said Mr Garside. "I can most certainly fill you in with a great deal of the facts about Willerby Grange, for I belong to the local Historical Society. To be able to research the history of this beautiful old building will be a wonderful opportunity to delve into real local history. You say you're leaving tomorrow?"

"Yes, we must tie up the loose ends, so to speak, then we will be moving into our new home, probably in a couple of weeks or so," said Ben."

"Right then, Mr Bristow, that gives me time to get all our moles in the Society digging up as much information on the Grange as possible. I look forward to your return.

Here is my card, perhaps you could give me a ring when you get settled in the Grange." He turned to Celia. "Nice to meet you, and I hope you're looking forward to the move."

"Yes," said a strangely shy Celia. For some inexplicable reason she felt drawn to this softly spoken, seemingly well educated man. You couldn't possibly fail to notice those deep blue eyes, the greying hair and sideburns which suited this tall, well groomed man. What on earth was the matter with her? She had only just met this stranger, but she saw something in his eyes, too.

Ben's voice broke the spell. "Come on then, we'd better be making our way back to the Grange. There is much to do. We only have until tomorrow evening to sort out what furniture we are going to keep and what must be got rid of."

Alex Garside looked at Ben. "I'll be seeing you, Mr Bristow. By the time you come to live in Yorkshire, I will have all the information you require."

With that the family left the restaurant and made their way to the car.

"You're a bit quiet, Mum," said Jess.

Celia replied "I'm just thinking of all the sorting out regarding the number of rooms in the Grange," she said, but the truth was she didn't know how she felt, except to say that she had been unsettled by a handsome stranger.

They were soon back at the Grange. "I'm going across to the Coach House," said Ben. "I must ask Barnaby for his help."

He, Jess and Celia had discussed last evening what they must do regarding all the furniture. It had been decided that any item they wanted to keep would be labelled and they would ask Barnaby if he would like any of the rest; if not, it could go to a children's charity.

When Ben arrived at the Coach House, Barnaby let him in and the two men discussed in detail what was to be done. Barnaby agreed to give any help he could and his wife would be happy to help if wanted.

"OK," said a grateful Ben. "Come over when you're both ready."

So the mammoth task was started; room after room was gone through, labelled and sorted, and by the time Sunday evening arrived everyone was exhausted, but very relieved that the job had been well done. It was now six thirty in the evening, so the family decided to leave the sleeping bags at the Grange. The children had enjoyed their camping holiday, as Jack put it, so they travelled light back to Everbey, and arrived at about ten p.m.

They took Celia home first. "Thank you all for a lovely weekend," said a tired but happy Celia. She looked at the 'sold' sign on the notice in her front garden, and although she had lived happily in this lovely cottage for many years, she was now experiencing a pulling away. It was a sad feeling, tinged with betrayal, as if she were leaving Tom behind, but this was silly; Tom would want her to move on, for his memory would be with her wherever she went.

Celia busied herself with packing, ringing all the services: gas, electricity, phone company, in fact putting into order all she needed to make the move to Yorkshire as stress-free as possible. Likewise, the Bristows were similarly engaged, and eventually everything was packed into two removal vans with Montgomery and Hetty in a pet carrier, the latter being quite a struggle. Hetty was a big cat, and despite Jess trying to comfort the disgruntled big lump, she meowed nearly all the way to Yorkshire.

After almost three weeks since leaving the Grange, they were once again travelling to Yorkshire, to a beautiful new life in Willerby Grange, and what a life it was going to be.

CHAPTER FOUR
New Start, New Life

"Come on Hetty, we're here now," said Jess who had been concerned for her pet ever since the journey had begun.

"She'll be all right, love. Cats are resilient creatures," said Ben, for he knew how much the pets meant to Jess, "and all the family, really. When both pets find their bearings they'll be fine. It's an animal paradise here." Ben gave Jess a hug and it wasn't long before Montgomery was sniffing round the garden and orchard.

"Just look at him. He is in his element," said Jack, happy for his pet. "It's magic here," said the happy lad. "Can I go exploring, dad?"

"Off you go," said Ben, "but don't go out of the gate." The rest of the family went towards the big oak door and stepped inside their new home. Jess was carrying Hetty in the pet basket. She opened the lid, and in a flash the cat jumped out, and disappeared behind a kitchen dresser.

"Just leave her alone, love," said Ben. "She will come out when she's ready." Jess, not being sure about that statement, went towards where the cat had gone.

"How about I put the kettle on?" said Celia. "We could all do with a nice cup of tea, I'm sure."

"Does anybody fancy fish and chips?" said Ben.

"That would be lovely," said Celia.

"OK then," said Ben. "I'll pop to Axenby. It won't take me long. You coming, Alice?"

"Yes please, Dad," she answered. So off they went, to return in half an hour with delicious Yorkshire fish and chips. The removal vans had gone, and all their belongings had been put into the appropriate rooms.

Barnaby and Nora Sykes had done a wonderful job getting the Grange ready for the family's return: fires had been lit in every room, furniture not required had been disposed of (a local children's charity being very thankful for the gift), and all the main services had been connected.

"I'm so pleased that Barnaby and his wife are living in the Coach House. I suppose they must have been worried as to what would happen to them after Reuben Bristow died, and I'm glad you had that chat with Barnaby when we came for the weekend, Ben," said Jess.

"They do seem a decent pair, and I'm glad you asked Nora to come in every day and give you a hand. It's a big place and it will give you chance to get on with your writing, Jess."

"And I can start my water colour painting," said Celia. "It's an ideal place to do some landscape work. I can just imagine taking my easel and paints onto the cliff top. What a vista that will be!"

So their new life started in Willerby Grange, Alice attending the local grammar school and Jack the primary school, both in Axenbey. Barnaby continued with the gardening and Nora helped in the Grange most days. Montgomery and Hetty soon found their feet, and settled down very well, Hetty getting bigger than ever.

"I think she must be catching rabbits instead of mice," said Jess to Ben one day, who was now working from home most of the time.

"Working at home gives me the chance to learn some garden skills from Barnaby," Ben told Jess and Celia.

"Also I am beginning to learn some very interesting facts about the Bristow family. Mind you, Barnaby is a bit cagey. He was telling me this morning that he can remember me being born in 1942 during the Second World War. I was born on the family farm, and Barnaby said he could remember my father running out of the house shouting, 'It's a boy! It's a boy!' It seems my grandparents had owned the farm, and my father James and my mother Dora Jane, lived there, together with Reuben"

"Apparently my father and Reuben were twins. Something terrible happened between them. Something so awful in fact, that my mum and dad moved away to Everbey when I was about a year old.

"According to Barnaby this trouble between the brothers had gone on for years, and it was thought it was the contributing factor that had caused the early death of their mother, my grandmother. It has to be said however that I was adored by Reuben, and until my parents moved away, my Uncle Reuben doted on me, that was until his terrible accident."

Barnaby continued the tale. "Reuben was trimming branches from a large Blenheim apple tree when he fell, hitting his head very badly and breaking his leg in three places. He was in the local hospital for weeks, and when he eventually returned to the farm he was never the same."

"How do you mean?" said a very intrigued Ben.
The old man stopped suddenly. "I think the past is better left in the past." With that the old gardener had gone in the direction of the Coach House.

"I must find out what is the terrible secret," Ben said to Jess. "This is all part of the hurt that caused so much misery to my father and grandparents. I must find out and lay this ghost to rest once and for all."

"Are you sure, Ben?" said his wife. "Remember the old saying, 'Let sleeping dogs lie".

Ben in a worried voice answered.

"Yes, I know all that Jess, but we are starting a new life here. I need to get rid of anything that could hold us back. I must find out the truth."

Ben went to the Coach House and knocked on the door. Nora Sykes opened the door. "Come in, Mr Ben. We half expected you," said Nora.

"You know why I'm here then?" said Ben.

Barnaby came into the kitchen and Ben looked at the old gardener. He liked this Yorkshire man, who said what he thought; he was the salt of the earth.

"Now then, lad, if you are sure you want me to tell you, then I shall. Best get the wife to come over, then I can tell the story to you both."

He turned to Nora and said. "Can you go and fetch her, lass?" And when Nora had returned with Jess he began, "The story I'm going to tell thee is sad in its way, but it happened a long time ago. I'll tell it the best I can, lad," and Barnaby Sykes proceeded to unravel the mystery that had dogged the Bristow family for too many years.

"It all started way back when your dad and Uncle Reuben were at grammar school. A young lass by the name of Dora Jane Appleyard attended the same school and by 'eck, she was bonny. Well, she fell hook, line and sinker for your dad, and he fell for her, and it was obvious to anybody who knew them that they were meant for each other; for young as they were, a mature love was blossoming in their hearts. But there was a fly in the ointment. Reuben Bristow also fell deeply in love with Dora Jane Appleyard.

"Perhaps being twins, James and Reuben had a similar make up, which would account for them both falling for the same lass, but whereas James was gentle and quiet and rather shy by nature, Reuben was the opposite, loud and rather crude in speech. In fact, not the sort of person to interest Dora Jane. How could two brothers be so different?

"They were very similar in looks except for the eyes. James had the darkest blue, portraying a gentleness that came from within. Reuben, however, had a cold sort of look. Everyone who knew the boys were aware of the different natures. Your grandparents were put to shame by the antics of young Reuben…"

Ben interrupted, "How do you know all this? Have you known the Bristow family for a long time?"

Barnaby stopped and, looking at Ben, he said,

"Let me go back a bit further. My father met your grandfather when they were both in the army in France, in the First World War. According to the limited information I was able to glean from my father, the conditions out there were appalling.

Your grandfather was wounded in battle, and my father went to his aid and did what he could to help. Harry Bristow was in a field hospital for a long time, suffering from shell shock amongst other things, before being sent home. My father finished his time, was demobbed, then fell on hard times. Harry Bristow gave him a job on the farm and he met my mother in Axenby.

They both lived on the farm, and that's where I was born, and grew up."

Jess looked at Ben. "The story gets more fascinating by the hour. No wonder you know so much," she said to Barnaby.

"Aye, lass," he said, "but even I was to see and hear things I didn't really want to be a part of."

Ben, rather shocked by all Barnaby had to divulge, said "If it's anything to do with the Bristow family, do you think you could enlighten us?"

"Alright, Mr Ben," he replied. "I will do my best."

Dorothy M. Mitchell

CHAPTER FIVE
The Truth and Nothing but the Truth

"As I have already told you, my father and your
grandfather go back as far as the First World War, true
pals, but what happened during that terrible time was to
have a lasting effect on Harry Bristow. My earliest
recollection of the events on Apple Orchard farm go
back to my childhood. I would be about four years old
when your grandmother came knocking on our door.

"Lucas, come quick," she said. "I can't do anything with
him. He just won't stop screaming."

This sort of thing happened on a pretty regular basis. I
knew from an early age that Mr Bristow was poorly;
however, when I was about five years old your dad and
Uncle Reuben were born. They were almost identical.
Your dad was a gentle quiet boy, but Reuben was a
different kettle of fish, mischievous in the extreme. Your
dad got many a good hiding, taking the blame for one of
Reuben's pranks, but it was obvious that James loved
his wayward brother.

This way of life went on for a number of years, and I
always knew that Reuben took advantage of the fact
that his father was a sick man, his mother less and less
able to cope.

Then one fateful day Matilda found Harry slumped in the
barn, and came running for my father, but it was too
late. The inquest said he had suffered a massive heart
attack. Matilda tried to carry on, but she was worn out
and passed away within a few months of Harry's death.

"Your dad and Reuben were now eighteen years old, and joint owners of Apple Orchard farm. James asked my parents to stay on, and as I was also living and working on the farm, I was asked if I wanted to stay on. Well naturally, as it had been the only life I had known, or indeed wanted, I was happy to accept. Anyway, I had started walking out with Nora, a girl from just outside Axenby, so I would need secure employment in order to be able to ask the girl I loved to be my wife."

Barnaby sighed. "I wasn't the only one who was besotted with a beauty. Young James had loved a girl he met at grammar school, by the name of Dora Jane Appleyard."

Jess, enthralled by all Barnaby had told them, said "Oh Ben, isn't this all so romantic?" She had been quietly listening to all Barnaby had to say, and could sense a degree of emotion as he re-lived some memories that were part of his life.

Barnaby retorted "It wasn't all romantic, lass, some memories are a bit hard to take; but if I can continue.

Getting back to Dora Jane. As I say, James was so in love with her, and she with him. The trouble was Reuben also had feelings for Dora Jane, but she only had eyes for James. It was awful at times. Reuben would go to the pub, come home blind drunk, then he and James would end up fighting.

James always came off the worst, for he wasn't a fighter. Anyway, to cut a long story short, when James was twenty and Dora Jane eighteen they married at the local church. It was a lovely wedding, well attended. They came back to the farm, and started their married lives together. Reuben seemed to accept the inevitable and things were fine for a time.

"Then you came along, Mr Ben. By, but you were a bonny baby."

Jess turned to Barnaby. "You're making Ben blush," she said.

"Go on," said Ben, for he was learning truths from the past that he felt sure would be a salve for the future; for good or bad, he needed to know.

Barnaby continued. "Are you sure you want to know any more, Mr. Ben?" Ben nodded. "Yes, please continue Barnaby."

"Right, if you're sure Sir," said the old gardener.

"Reuben became so obsessed with you that when you were about a year old your mum and dad felt they had to get away. Couldn't stand the cloying interference of Reuben any longer. James, your dad, got a position as manager on a fruit farm in the Cotswolds, Everby. The place that became your home."

Nora came into the kitchen. "How about a cup of tea? You must be parched."

Barnaby looked at his wife. "Aye, lass, we could all do with one, cos it takes some telling does this tale." Barnaby drained his cup, then said, "Right, to continue." Ben nodded.

"James kept in touch with my parents. Letters regularly went back and forth between them. Reuben, however, was like a bear with a sore head. Nothing would placate him. My mum did her best, but to no avail, he became very morose and continued in this vein until the fateful day of his accident.

By this time, both my parents had passed away and I was married to Nora. She cooked for Reuben and looked after the house, while I got on with the farm work." Barnaby stopped speaking.

"Go on," said Ben.

Barnaby continued. "It was me as found him. It was a terrible sight. He was at the bottom of the old Blenheim tree, bleeding like a stuck pig, the old band-saw beside him and covered in dead branches. It looked as though he had been cutting out dead wood from the top of the tree and he must have slipped.

He was in hospital for weeks, broke his leg in three places, and bashed his head badly. I got in touch with your folks and James made a couple of trips to visit his brother, but Reuben was unconscious for a long time and wasn't aware of anything. When he did eventually go home it was obvious that he could no longer manage the farm. It was also evident that his brain had been badly damaged during his accident, because he kept asking for his son, and despite being assured repeatedly that he didn't have a son, Reuben was convinced in his sick mind that you were his boy."

Ben, shocked by this revelation, said very quietly,

"Good grief! Poor Uncle Reuben! I didn't expect that, Barnaby."

The old gardener carried on. "And that's not all, Mr Ben, somehow, and nobody quite knows how, Mr Reuben sold Apple Tree Orchard farm, and bought Willerby Grange with the proceeds, knowing full well that he was no longer able to run the farm. The only way he could have done it was to forge your dad's signature on the documents. For although he was by now mentally ill, he was astute enough to have got away with it. James was mortified and in the end, after many arguments between the brothers, it was apparent that James was weary of the fight, and I don't need to tell you that your father passed away a sad man.

His abiding comfort being Dora Jane, and you, for I know that the love your parents had for each other never diminished."

"How can you know all these facts?" said Ben to the man who had just told him so much sad Bristow family history.

"Well, Mr Ben, our families go back a long way, intertwined since the First World War. I was a confidante to your dad for many a long year, as was my father before me. We were never treated as menials. Your father was a good man, I held him in the highest esteem, and as for Reuben, well I couldn't feel the same respect for him, but he did keep me and Nora on. Mind you, he needed us, so it wasn't completely unselfish.

"I'm too old now to go looking for another job, so Nora and I are grateful that you are keeping us on."

With that Ben stood up and said, "We must be going, or else the rest of the family will think we have got lost." Ben held out his hand to the man who had given him what he had needed to know for so many years. Barnaby took it.

"I hope I haven't upset you too much lad" said Barnaby.

"I needed to know, Barnaby. Thank you so much," said Ben.

Jess, sensing the turmoil in her husband's mind, took hold of Ben's hand.

They said goodbye to Nora and Barnaby, left the Coach House, and walked across to the Grange.

"Oh, there you are," said Celia. "Lunch is almost ready."

Ben excused himself, saying, "I won't be a moment."

Jess watched this man she adored walk out of the kitchen. He went in the direction of the staircase. She followed Ben into their bedroom, and gently closed the door, looking into his moist eyes. Ben Bristow spoke in a broken voice.

"Jessica, I feel I could cry for a month"

She took him into her arms, and tears that had been locked away for years flooded his being. "At last Jess, I know the sad truth, and what a truth it is. How can one family cope with such heartbreak? I can see all sides of the situation. Love and hate are part of the same emotion. I feel so deeply for all my family's trauma."

Ben was speaking to Jess through sobbing choking tears, and as Jess held this gentle man, the man whom she loved so deeply, she felt that this was the start of healing. It was time to put all the events of the past that caused so much pain to so many as far away as possible.

"Ben, will you come for a walk with me?" she pleaded.
Ben looked at his Jess through the tears. He nodded his acceptance.

They went downstairs.
"Mum, will you keep our lunch warm?" she said. "Ben and I need to go out for a little while."
"Can we come?" said Jack and Alice.
"No, dears, we won't be long," their mother replied.

Jess and Ben walked out to the garden, through the gate that led to the path, down to the beach. The tide was lapping the sand and it made a gentle soothing sound as it licked the shingle. Seagulls were calling their melancholy cry. Jess took Ben's hand and they walked to the edge of the water.
"Sweetheart," she said, "let the gentle waves carry the pain far out to sea. You don't need it any more. It can't hurt you any more. We have a lovely new life to live in this beautiful place, and everything is going to be fine from now on. I feel we have turned a corner."
Ben held Jess tight in his arms, and whispered, "I love you so much."

They stood letting the waves lap around their feet, and Ben understood what his lovely wife meant. It would take a little time, but he was determined that they would all benefit from this move to the East Coast of Yorkshire which had so much to offer. Willerby Grange was situated overlooking a bay; to either side, the grass-topped cliffs sloped down to a secluded golden beach.

Jess had remarked to Ben on an earlier occasion just how private this beach was. Ben looked at his beloved Jess, saying, "We will make it work, love, for now I know the truth. What better place to begin our new lives?"

He took her hand. "Just look at the Grange from this angle. Whoever built that magnificent house knew exactly what they were doing."

They stood hand in hand gazing up at the Grange. "Yes," said Jess, with the cliffs curling round on either side. "We are completely private."

They walked towards the steps. "It's like the old house is keeping guard," she added. "Ben, this place is steeped in history."

Ben smiled at this woman who meant the world to him. He smiled. "I bet our lunch is dried up by now," he said as Alice and Jack came running towards them.

"Gran gave your lunch to Montgomery, and Hetty," said Jack. Celia, overhearing the children, said "Come on, you two. Stop telling tales!"

"Don't worry, I prepared a salad for you both for when you returned."

Celia had felt the pain her son-in-law was struggling with, and when they put her in the picture later, she heaved a sigh of relief. Now they could all move on, for with time Ben would be free of the family pain that had caused so much anguish.

CHAPTER SIX
Settling In, Making Friends

"What on earth are we going to do with all this fruit?
The trees are just laden with so many different varieties;
Bramley and Newton are lovely cookers; Cox and lovely
William pears for eating!"

Celia was in her element. Barnaby had just come into
the orchard. "Ee, missus. It's a bumper crop this year
and no mistake."

"What usually happens?" said Celia to the gardener.

"I'm afraid Mr Reuben never bothered with it. He let us
have what we wanted, and he would ask Nora to make
him an apple pie on occasion, but that was about all.
The fruit would just be allowed to rot. Lads from round
about would chance their arm, but if he caught them he
would box their ears."

Celia was fired with enthusiasm. "We must do
something about it then," she said.

"We just can't let all this lovely fruit go to waste." Celia
was quick to have a word with Ben and Jess. "Barnaby
tells me that there is a brick store room at the far side of
the orchard which hasn't been used for years. How
about we put it to use again?"

"Well," said Jess, "with such a bumper crop, it would be
a shame not to use such bounty."

"It's coming up to Harvest Festival at school, we could
take some," said Alice eagerly. "I expect Jack would
take some fruit to his school as well."

So it was also decided to ask the vicar of St Peter's
Church if they would like some fruit for their forthcoming
Harvest Festival. "How about the elderly in these parts?"

said Celia. "Shall I ask Barnaby and Nora, for they will know, and perhaps we could get some of the young folks to help us pick? We will never manage all these trees by ourselves."

The old man was full of interest. "Shall I ask around?" he said, seemingly more than pleased that things had really improved since Mr Ben and family had moved into the Grange.

Well, what activity, ladders, baskets, people scurrying all over the orchard. "Isn't this fun?" said Alice to Jess as they drank a glass of home made lemonade. "I didn't think all these people would come."

Montgomery was in his element, for he liked a lot of fuss, and he was getting plenty. He was patted, cuddled, and best of all, ham sandwiches and sausages were being passed around. If he gave that special cute look, he could be sure of a few titbits.

Friendships were formed, and when the day finally came to a close, the store-room was full and the orchard was well picked. It had been a wonderful day all round.

When all the helpers had gone home and the family were sitting enjoying a cup of tea, it was twilight.

"Has everyone recovered now?" It was Ben asking the question. They had all given it their best, from early morning to a few moments ago.

It had been hectic; Celia and Jess providing refreshments, the children picking and playing around the orchard with their friends, Montgomery running around in jubilation at all the activity (he just loved people, mainly because, the more people, the more juicy morsels. He was one crafty dog!).

"Ben, it has been a wonderful day," said Jess, looking up at Ben, and she thought to herself, "It's as though a great weight has been lifted from his shoulders." The pain in his eyes had gone, to be replaced by an eagerness for life.

Ben held his Jess close to him and said,

"I've got to go to Everby, love. If I set off first thing, I can be back home by evening." Back home, Ben thought to himself; that feels wonderful. "It's a bit of business I have to see to tie up the loose ends, so to speak."

They kissed, and Ben was on the road at first light. He had to see old Josh Webb about a bit of work he had done for him, but that wasn't the main reason for this visit. Ben arrived in his old home town at ten thirty. It looked the same, but it wasn't home any more.

After his visit with Josh Webb, he stayed outside the churchyard, sat for a few moments, stepped out of the car and walked slowly to where his mum and dad were laid to rest. He knelt down, by the grave: DORA JANE BRISTOW, DIED AUGUST 10th 1948 JAMES BRISTOW DIED JAN 1952 REST IN PEACE.

Ben touched the lettering and said quietly, "Mum, Dad, just came to let you both know that now you can rest in peace. I am back home where I should be. I love you both. Rest now." And having visited the resting place of the mum and dad who had shaped his life and given so much of themselves to him as a young boy, he prayed that wherever they were, angels would be keeping watch over them, for they would always be special to him.

Then Ben walked out of the peaceful churchyard and sat in his car for a moment, before he was back on the road going home.

CHAPTER SEVEN
History Past and in the Making

Ben turned into the drive at Willerby Grange, the time now six twenty, and Jess and the family met him. "You made good time," said Jess, taking Ben's hand. "All right, love?"

Ben smiled; "I couldn't be better, sweetheart. How about we all go down to the beach? Come on, Montgomery."

Jack was all for it. "I'll race you," said Alice, and with that the children charged through the gate.

"Be careful down the path," called Celia who was always worried that one of the children would go flying, as she put it, but oblivious of her warning they were on the sand in no time at all. The autumn sun was low in the sky, sitting on the sea as Jack put it. He and Alice played ball, while Montgomery made a thorough investigation of a pile of seaweed on the sand, before deciding it was worth a good wee.

Ben and Jess strolled hand in hand along the shore, while Celia picked up shells. "Oh by the way, Ben, I almost forgot to tell you that Mr Garside called this morning. It seems The Historical Society has managed to dig up a great deal of history on Willerby Grange. He said would you ring him when it's convenient for him to call."

"That sounds interesting," said Ben, who had been waiting to hear this news, and when they returned home he rang Mr Garside.

"Hello, Mr Garside, I understand you have some news for us regarding the history of Willerby Grange."

Alex Garside answered the phone.

"Thanks for ringing back, Mr Bristow. Yes indeed, I can hardly wait to see you; the amount of information on Willerby Grange is so exciting. Our members were absolutely astonished as more and more facts were uncovered. I can assure you Mr Bristow that you will be flabbergasted."

"That sounds intriguing. When can you come to visit?"

"How about tomorrow evening?" said a very excited Alex Garside, making it a firm date.

"Did you hear that, Jess? Mr Garside is coming tomorrow evening, and by the sound of what he was saying, we are in for a good chat."

The historian arrived laden with books and papers and the family met him with much excitement. After the usual niceties, shaking hands, and making their guest welcome, the books and papers were laid out on the kitchen table and Alex Garside began; "You are already aware that the Grange was built in the reign of Elizabeth 1st – 1570, to be exact - however, what we discovered was that The Grange was actually built by Benjamin Charles Bristow, and was originally called 'Bristow Grange', as the Bristow family were at that time very wealthy and owned a fleet of fishing boats. They employed dozens of men at their yard in Hull."

Ben sat dumbstruck and said, "I can hardly take this in."

Alex Garside smiled. "I'm not surprised," he said, "and there is so much more. Shall I continue? The Bristow family lived at the Grange for many years. They were known to be staunch Royalists, so when in the Civil War in the 1640s Royalists were being hunted and put to death, the Bristow family fled to France, in fear for their lives. Then Oliver Cromwell came to power, and placed one of his officers named Captain Willerby in Bristow Grange, and he promptly changed the name to Willerby Grange. The Bristow family came back to England in 1661 and bought Apple Orchard farm, So you can see that the farm goes back a long way in the history of your family."

"My goodness," said Ben. "I'm having trouble taking all this in."

"Ben," Celia butted in, "this is all sounding very intriguing, but it was obvious when we came to live at the Grange that it was a place steeped in history; yet to be told that the Bristow family built it and lived here all those years ago is absolute magic. How romantic, but can we ever know just how hard it must have been for them to leave their beautiful home? Do you think that the sighing noises we sometimes hear in this old place are the voices of your ancestors' anguish?"

Alex Garside looked at this woman who had made an impression on him when they'd first met. "That's an interesting point, but I doubt you will ever know the answer to that question!"

Celia smiled and looked away, as Alex Garside turned to Ben, and said, "We managed to get a lot more information from the Reverend Paul Jeffries. Apparently church records show that from the time Willerby Grange was built the Bristow family were very involved in church activities until they had to flee to France. Births marriages and deaths are all written in the Church ledgers. Then there is a gap of a number of years before the family name was once again to be found in the register of St Peter's Church."

"Ben, we must go and visit Mr Jeffries and thank him," said Celia.

"Yes, we will do, love," Ben replied.

Alex Garside continued to give dates and times of interesting events that were relevant to the Bristow family. Ben liked this quiet unassuming man, as Alex went on, "Willerby Grange has had a chequered history. In the 18th century it had been a doctors' surgery, a private school, and then in the 19th century it was bought by the mayor of Axenbey, and sold to the owner of a woollen mill. It then lay empty until your uncle Reuben bought it. There are a few minor details, but that is the history of the Grange up to the present day. I have been asked by our members to say a hearty thanks to all of you for the privilege of delving into what has been a most fabulous history lesson, but despite our in-depth work we were unable to uncover any references to idle talk that abounds in these parts of pirates, hidden treasure, and the like. It's a load of humbug as far as I'm concerned, but you know what people are." With that, Alex Garside stood up and said finally, "Well, Ben, I have enjoyed relaying to you all the findings of our little group."

He shook hands with the family. "Thanks, Alex," said Ben. "You certainly kept Alice and Jack quieter than I have ever known them." Everyone smiled.

"Please feel free to call any time. Perhaps you would come for a meal one evening and bring your wife along," said Jess. She liked Alex. "Thank you so much Jess, I would love to accept your kind offer, but my wife died three years ago. She was in hospital for a long time, so I will come alone."

He left and the family fell quiet.

"Oh, the poor man," said Jess. "How were we supposed to know?"

"We couldn't, love," said Ben, sad for this nice man. Something told him that he was going to become a friend, not just to him, but to the whole family.

CHAPTER EIGHT
Fireworks and Flowers

"Jack, will you bring the wheelbarrow over here?" said Ben.

"OK, Dad," Jack replied.
"And don't keep jumping on that pile of wood, Jack. I've stacked it half a dozen times already. If you want a bonfire you'd better start helping."
Celia and Jess were really getting stuck in. It had been decided that they would celebrate November the fifth with an enormous bonfire and invite friends they had made since living at the Grange. The weather by now had turned cold and misty and the mists at times were dense owing to the close proximity of the sea, which, instead of being calm and a green blue colour, was stormy and rolling. High waves crashed along the shore, at times almost covering the beach below. At other times, the fog was so thick you couldn't see a hand in front of your face.
"I will be glad when it's bonfire night. It will be warm with the fire blazing. Do you think we will be able to have roasted potatoes? I love them when they go all black."

"You'll have to ask Dad, Jack," said Celia, trying to keep warm. They had all been out in the orchard for the best part of the day, collecting wood, clearing debris and generally preparing the grounds for the forthcoming bonfire party the following evening. "It's a good job you two are on school holidays, or else I don't know if we would have coped."

Celia knew just how to get the best out of her grandchildren. She put her arms around them and Jack beamed, while Alice cuddled up to her gran. "Now come on, let's get finished. Your mum and I have a great deal to do tomorrow. We will be cooking all day. Do you think you will be able to help Dad and Barnaby put up the lanterns in the trees? Away from the fire, mind!"

Alice and Jack felt important. "Of course we can, Gran."

"That's settled then. Come on into the house, both of you. Where's Montgomery? He was chasing a rabbit last time I saw him. Go and fetch him, Jack. There's a good lad."

When they were all safely indoors, Celia served the stew she had prepared earlier in the slow cooker. She gave a portion to Hetty and Montgomery; my goodness, it didn't take them long to wolf that down. Anybody would think they had been working hard all day. Ben had watched the pets clear their dishes of every morsel, and remarked how well both the pets had settled down, as indeed had all the family; and tomorrow was going to be a very special day, November 5th. 1979 would be the best Bonfire Night any of them had enjoyed.

"How many people did we reckon would come?" asked Ben.

"About thirty, including all the children and parents. Did you remind everyone to keep their pets indoors?" asked Jess.

"Of course I did," said Ben, putting his arm around his wife. "Now why don't you sit down, and I'll make a cup of tea? You and Celia have been working all day, cooking and cleaning as though we're expecting royalty!"

"I know, Ben, but I just want everything to be right," said Jess.

"It will be perfect, love," Ben replied.

It was early evening and the garden and orchards looked lovely.

Tables and chairs had been dotted about between the trees, and lanterns danced in the branches. "It looks just like fairyland," said Alice to her gran.

Down in the bottom field well away from the Grange and trees the huge bonfire stood in all its splendour. "When can we light it?" asked Jack.

"When everybody arrives," said his dad. "How about you and I going down to the gate to meet our guests?"

Celia busied herself putting final touches to the tables. The soup was simmering on the stove, and Jess was breaking the toffee they had made earlier. She couldn't resist a little taste. Nothing quite like home made toffee! The bread rolls were piled onto trays.

The Reverend Paul Jeffries was first to arrive. "My goodness! Somebody has been busy!" he exclaimed, rubbing his hands together. "Everything looks wonderful, and what a lovely evening for the festivities."

People started to arrive in quick succession and soon Willerby Grange was a hive of activity. Ben shook hands with Alex Garside. "Glad you could make it, Alex," he said, then the bonfire was lit. Rockets whizzed skyward with rapturous cheers from children and adults alike. Potatoes were thrown into the embers; Catherine wheels and sparklers, Roman candles and jumping jacks fizzed and crackled. Fingers were sticky from toffee that went down a treat.

"Just look at Jack's face," said Jess to Mrs Harper, mother of George, one of Jack's school friends. George was likewise displaying a black mouth and hands where the pair had enjoyed a charcoal potato from the bonfire. Mrs Irene Harper had become quite a regular visitor. She and Jess had formed a friendship since Jack had been a pupil at the village school, and George and Jack took to each other straight away.

It was apparent to Jack that young George wasn't very happy, probably because he was on the plump side and had to wear glasses. They put the boy at a disadvantage, and consequently he was rather shy and withdrawn, whereas Jack was quite the opposite. He liked this boy who had shown him kindness on his first day at the new school, and as time went on, Jack sort of looked after his new friend. "Just look at the pair of them, Mrs Bristow. My, but it does my heart good to see them together. I've worried so over George, but your lad has brought him out."

Jess felt a glow of pride. Her son was well adjusted and happy in his new life, as indeed were the rest of the family. Also the friendship she and Irene had formed was of the lasting kind. "I do wish you would call me Jess," she said.

Her new friend looked at this woman who had brought something special into her life. "All right, Jess. It's just that I am of the old school, rather old-fashioned." They smiled at each other and walked over to what remained of the bonfire where the Reverend Jefferies was speaking.

"How about three hearty cheers for Jess, Celia, and Ben for this wonderful evening, and in the dying embers of the bonfire, how about a singsong to bring the evening to a close? I see Tom Baines has brought his accordion, so come on, let's have a few of the old ones."

Tom started playing, "If you were the only girl in the world, and I were the only boy", and a beautiful baritone voice started up. It was Alex Garside. "Jess, isn't it wonderful?" said Irene. "When Helen was alive they were both members of St Peter's choir, but apart from the Historical Society, Alex is quite a recluse now."

"You know him then?" said Jess, looking at her new friend.

"Yes, we have been neighbours for a number of years. A lovely man. He and Helen were devoted. She was very ill for a long time; TB, died in a Sanatorium about three years ago. Bill and I did what we could, and my hubby tried to take him out of himself, but it was hard work. Anyway, of late he seems to be coming out of the grief, and it's so nice to see the change in him."

After cheering and clapping for a song well sung, Alex asked everyone to join in with a few more of the old favourites. Reverent Jeffries brought the evening to a close with a reminder of the forthcoming Christmas party at the Church Hall, with a request for volunteers to help in any way they could, i.e., providing and preparing food, and a request for anyone who could do a turn. By 10:15 most of the guests had gone home, and Ben and Barnaby were dousing the ashes of the bonfire. All the children had done a wonderful job of clearing the rubbish into sack bags that Barnaby had provided.

"I don't know about anyone else, but I could do with a lovely cup of tea," said Jess, putting an arm around her mum. "Come on, I'll make you one. You've worked hard." Celia smiled.

Just then Alex came from the orchard. "Look who I found," he said. In his arms, fast asleep, was a very grubby Jack.

Just look at him, Ben," Jess smiled at her hubby. "He's had a smashing day."

Ben took his son into his arms. "Thank you Alex, this one is going straight to his bed as he is. He can have a bath in the morning, Are you going to stay for a cup of tea? Jess is just making one."

"I would love one," said Alex.

"Come on in then," said Ben, and Alex followed the family indoors.

"Have you enjoyed the day, Celia?" said Alex, looking at Celia, and thinking how tired she appeared. "You must all have worked for days to achieve such a wonderful evening."

"Oh yes, it's been hard work, but well worth the effort, and it has been lovely to meet the people of the village. Jess has made friends with a nice lady, a neighbour of yours I believe, Irene Harper."

Alex took a sip of tea. "So you know all about me then?"

"Well, only that she and her husband had been quite concerned for you during your time of loss," said Celia.

"They are both kindness itself," Alex replied.

Celia wondered if she'd caused any pain to this gentle man and said, "I hope that I haven't upset you, Alex, by broaching a subject that must be very hurtful to you?"

"No," he answered. "Don't worry, and to be honest I thought at one time that the pain would never leave me, but the old saying that time is a healer is true." Alex stood up. "Anyhow, it's time I was off." He took Celia's hand; they exchanged a glance of knowing. Celia felt a warm glow stir deep within which they both felt.

"Well, are you off then, Alex?" said Ben.

"Yes, Ben, and thanks for a lovely evening. Will you be going to the church hall next week? Paul always expects the village to put on a good do for Christmas and, of course, we all oblige. He's a good sort. If you have a good singing voice he will be roping you in for the choir."

Ben looked at Celia. "What about you? We can hear your dulcet tones in the bathroom," he joked.

Jess smiled. "Go on," she said. "It will do you good."

Celia could feel a flush coming to her face. What on earth was the matter with her? She felt like a teenager again, but she knew, oh yes, she knew. Alex took his leave, after accepting an invitation to come to dinner the following Saturday. Then the family cleared away the supper pots, and went to bed.

Just after light next day Barnaby arrived at the side door with a barrow load of blocks. "It's getting cold now, Mr Ben. I kept these back when I had been collecting wood for last night's bonfire. I thought they would be ideal for your fireplaces. There are plenty more good logs in the barn; enough to see you comfortably through the coldest winter, and by 'eck, we get some cold 'uns in these parts. I'm just about to bag up the ashes from the fire. They make good compost for the garden. Roses come up a treat, and the rhubarb."

Ben asked the gardener if he required any help. "No, it's a mucky job, Mr Ben, but thanks anyway," and with that Barnaby disappeared around the corner and got busy with the task in hand.

Ben shut the door, rubbing his hands together, with "My, but it's getting cold!" He was aware of the icy blast of wind coming in from the sea. He had remarked to Jess the previous night when they had been looking out over the crashing waves from their bedroom window, just how awesome the ocean could be, but also how privileged he felt that they were able to watch the power of the water at such close quarters.

Alice and Jack came running round the side of the orchard, shouting. "We've been watching Barnaby put all the ashes into sack bags. He looks a bit mucky" said Jack.

"That's a bit of Yorkshire, if you like," commented their father. "Come on in and have a warm drink." The children clambered in, their red cheeks looking the picture of health. Ben smiled. "This is the life all right," he said to himself.

Saturday morning came around and the butcher arrived, wanting to know if his meat was all right. Jess came into the kitchen. "Fred, what a lovely joint of beef. It will certainly look good on our dining table this evening."

Six thirty came around and the table was laid. The fire in the dining room was blazing, while from the kitchen the aroma of roast beef cooking in the big oven teased the nostrils. A beautiful arrangement of flowers adorned the centre of the dining table, and Jess and Celia were about to start setting out the cutlery, the best for this occasion, when Jack came charging into the dining room. "Gran, I can't find dad."

"He's just gone upstairs to get ready," said Celia. "Whatever is it?"

"Will you ask him to come into the big sitting room when he comes down?" Jack replied.

"My word you do look excited, Jack. Can we come?"

"If you like, Gran, but I don't think you will know." Puzzled by her grandson's actions she followed him into the large sitting room, closely followed by Ben, who, summoned by an equally excited Alice, had quickly hurried downstairs to see what the commotion was all about.

"Here, Dad," said young Jack, standing inside the enormous fireplace with his torch shining up the chimney. "Look here, Dad."

Intrigued, Ben went over to investigate just what his son was so interested in. He took the torch and looked up the chimney. As his eyes became used to the dark, he saw what Jack was excited about. "Well, would you believe it!" he exclaimed.

"Why? What are they, Dad?"

"Well, son, years ago before chimney sweeps came on the scene - mind you I'm going back a long time, probably as far back as when the Grange was built in 1570, cruel days in lots of ways - they used to send little boys as young as you up chimneys like these to clean them; and all those pegs that you see inside were used for the boys to climb on. Sometimes the fireplaces were still hot and a number of the little sweeps were burned, even killed in some cases."

"We learned about that in school and I think it's so sad. Poor little boys."

Alice seemed genuinely upset about the thought of the suffering these little boys must have endured, while Ben was trying to get a better look. He put his hand above him and grabbed hold of the top of the inside behind the shelf. He felt something on some sort of a ledge and pulled it towards him. "It looks like a key," he said, and brought the article into the daylight. It was covered in soot, thick soot. "Could be decades old," he commented.

"Can I hold it, Dad?" said Jack.

Ben placed the key into his son's hand. "Wow! Isn't it heavy?" exclaimed Jack. It was indeed a very old key; about four inches long with an ornate petal shaped top, similar to a fleur de lys. "How long do you think it's been there?"

"Hard to say," said his dad. Ben was intrigued, as were the rest of the family.

"Let me go and wash all the soot and grime away," said Jess, and having done this, she held the key in her hand saying, "My, but this surely is very old."

Jack, having followed his mother, shouted, "Come on, let's try all the doors and cupboards and see which the key fits."

Alice said, "Isn't this exciting? A bit like Cinderella and the glass slipper." The rest of them laughed but could see the similarity to the fairy story.

Jack in a theatrical voice uttered "Whichever lock this key fits…"

"Oh, come on, let's get started," said Celia, eager and fascinated with the whole idea. "It has to fit somewhere."

They set off and every door and cupboard lock was tried, but to no avail. "It just doesn't fit anything," Ben said to a rather disappointed family. "Never mind, it was like a treasure hunt and we did have fun. And because the key has been on that ledge inside the fireplace for goodness knows how long, how about I hang it on the hook we found at the side of the fireplace?"

Everyone nodded their approval and the deed was done. "Come on," said Celia. "It's time to get ready for dinner. Alex will be here shortly."

"Oh, goody," said Jack. For since meeting the historian the children had become very fond of him; but, of course, they weren't the only ones. Ben and Jess liked this charming new friend, and as for Celia, well she was wearing her new lilac dress, black wedge shoes, and black stole which complimented the frock.

The guest arrived and was greeted by Ben. "My, but you've brought some inclement weather with you Alex. Come on in by the fire."

"Evening, Ben," said Alex. "It's a cold one."

The two friends shook hands. "Come on, dinner is almost ready," said Jess. The two men followed Jess into the impressive dining room, where an inviting fire of logs crackled in the hearth.

"What a lovely bouquet of flowers you've brought, Alex," said Jess, as the visitor handed her the arrangement. Just then Celia entered the room and Alex took from the arrangement of chrysanthemums and carnations one single pale mauve carnation and gave it to the lady who had captured his heart. Celia blushed and smiled her thanks, attaching the token of affection securely to her brooch.

Jess, noticing the flush on her mum's cheeks, smiled as they sat enjoying the roast beef dinner. Ben and the family told Alex about the sooty key Ben had found inside one of the fireplace earlier that day. Jack asked if he could go and get it. "After dinner, Jack," his dad replied.

Following an excellent meal and while they enjoyed coffee, Alex examined the key. "From what I know, I would say it's about 16th century," he said.

"Why does it have all those holes in it?" asked Jack.

"Well, young man, because the key is so old and we presume that by the looks of it it's been on the ledge where your dad found it for all those years. Soot will have eaten into the iron causing it to become pitted, making the holes."

So with much discussion and wondering about the purpose of the mystery key, it was decided that for the time being anyway it could sit in the place of honour on the old hook on the fireplace from whence it came.

"But it must belong to a lock somewhere," said Jack.

CHAPTER NINE
Christmas at Willerby Grange 1979

"No darling, we don't want paper chains in the kitchen. It isn't the place for them."

"But, Mum, it would look Christmassy." Jack was full of it.

"No, Jack. Not the kitchen. Why don't you go and help Dad and Gran? I am sure they could do with another pair of hands. They are busy decorating the dining room and hall."

"Well, can I put paper chains up there then, Mum?"

"Jack, for goodness sake go and find your sister and see what you can both do to help," said Jess.

Celia could hear Jack and shouted, "Come on, young man. Alice is in the dining room with us. Your dad is just about to start decorating the tree, and he's asking for you. He needs your help."

With that Jack ran into the dining room feeling rather important. Ben smiled. Celia had worked her magic once more, Jess thought. "Ah, Jack" Just the boy I want." Ben was about to climb the ladder in order to reach the highest branches of the Christmas tree. Over his shoulder he was carrying coloured paper chains and baubles. "Now Jack, I need you to hold the bottom of the ladder as tight as you can."

The lad beamed. "OK, Dad," he replied, and so fervent activity carried on in this vein for the family's first Christmas at the Grange. It was a week before Christmas Day and Willerby Grange was buzzing. Decorations were all in place and Barnaby had made sure there would be sufficient logs to keep the fires burning.   The order had gone to Fred the butcher: goose and pork for the Christmas feast, while Jess and Celia had made enough Christmas cake and puddings to feed the village, according to Ben.

While the inside of the house was cosy and warm, the weather outside was turning bitterly cold. The snow that had previously fallen soft as a blanket was now frozen hard, and Jack had made a slide along one of the unused paths. "Boys will be boys; it's like a sheet of glass," said a concerned Celia. "Just you be careful and make sure Montgomery doesn't get on it either. You know he likes playing in the snow, but if he gets on that lethal slide he could break a leg."

"OK Gran," said Jack, trying his best to be as good as he could. He secretly still believed in Santa Claus but he knew some of his friends at school didn't believe, and he wasn't going to be made a laughing stock, so he kept that information to himself. Well, that is except for Montgomery, and Jack knew full well that the secret was quite safe with his best pal.

Christmas Eve Santa would be coming to Willerby Grange and he would know which chimney to come down, because Jack had written to him and told him.

Then Christmas Eve finally arrived, and as Alex walked in he commented on the decorations. "My, oh my! Don't the decorations look lovely," he exclaimed. He had been invited to spend the festive time with the family who had taken him to their hearts and he had grown to love the old Grange. Being involved with this lovely family, Willerby Grange had wound itself into the fabric of his being - due to the fact that a certain lady had touched his lonely heart, something he had thought impossible until that fateful day in the restaurant in Axenby. Was it only a few months ago? He had been walking on air ever since.

"You're covered in snow," said Ben as he let him in.

"Yes, it's started again," Alex replied.

Ben shook hands with his friend and told him the family were waiting. "Look who's arrived," said Ben. "Where's that hot toddy you were making? This chap is frozen." Celia and the rest of the family walked in, with Jess carrying a tray. "Here you are, Alex. Get that down you. It's my special warming rum and hot lemonade."

Alex took the glass and smiled at Celia. "It must be good if you made it, my dear," he said and everyone smiled. "This is going to be the best Christmas ever."

"I thought home-made soup and rolls would be all right for this evening's meal," said Jess, amused at the apparent romance that seemed to be blossoming between her mum and Alex. She and Ben were happy about it, for Celia had been a widow for a long time now. Jess knew from what her mum had confided in her that Celia had struggled with a feeling of guilt. "But, Mum, there really is no need for you to feel that way," Jess had assured her in an earlier chat the two had on the subject. "Dad would be happy for you, and Alex is such a lovely fellow. The children are very fond of him and children know. Believe me, Mum, everything is fine."

"Any more soup Mum?" asked Jack.

"My goodness, it didn't take you long to clean your bowl," said Jess as she ladled another portion into her son's dish.

"You know how much I love your soup, Mum," he replied. "It looks like it," said Alice, "judging by the load you've got down your jumper."

Everyone smiled as Jack tucked into his second helping. Then he asked, "Can I have some for Montgomery?"

"You'll have him as fat as a pudding if you keep on giving him titbits," said Ben, looking at his son and thinking that the children had really settled down so well to their new life in Yorkshire. "Go on then. Just a drop in his own bowl."

The meal was finished with everyone saying how much they had enjoyed it, and after coffee and mince pies Ben got up from the table and walked over to the window. "It's stopped snowing," he said. "Anyone feel like a walk down to the beach?"

"Yes please, Dad" came the reply from Alice and Jack.

"Get your boots on then and wrap up warm," said their father, and they set off trudging and laughing towards the far end of the orchard. Snow was piled up on top of the gate that led to the path down to the beach.

"Be very careful how you go," said Celia, who always worried about this path at the best of times, and once on the beach they stood and looked at a wonderland. A full moon shone a beam of silver light onto a cold, quiet sea. Snow on the beach was as it fell - new and untouched. Where the moonlight kissed the pure white snow it sparkled like diamonds, glistening and gleaming like a fantasia of jewels.

"It's like a wonderland," said Alice, enthralled.

"And it's a bit like Santa's grotto," said Jack in a hushed voice quietly to himself. He didn't want his sister knowing that he still believed in Father Christmas. She probably would be all right, but it was best to keep it to himself. Well, except for Gran, for he had an idea that she believed in Santa.

The family walked along the snow-clad beach for a little while and Jack threw a few snowballs into the sea till his dad said, "I think it's time we made our way back."

"Yes, your dad is right," said Jess. "Time is marching on and we still have lots to do before the big day tomorrow."

They trudged back towards the house with Ben going in front, then the children, and Jess following, with Celia and Alex hand in hand bringing up the rear.

Celia thought how comfortable her hand felt in the one that held hers as they reached the gate leading back into the orchard. In the near distance singing could be heard; "Silent Night, Holy Night".

"How lovely," said Jess to the rest. "It sort of finishes off a wonderful day." The singers were just entering the drive: five children from the village, ranging in age from about six to fifteen. "That was lovely," said Celia, and the rest nodded their approval. "Would you all like to come in for a warm and a mince pie?"

"Yes please!" came the reply.

After the singers had said their farewell it was time for Alice and Jack to go to bed, so after a hot milk drink, Celia tucked them both in with a kiss. "Goodnight. Sleep tight. See you both in the morning," but she knew full well that one certain young man wouldn't be going to sleep yet a while.

Morning came and they were greeted by, "He's been! He's been!" Jess and Ben were awakened by a very excited Jack. Montgomery, sensing something good must be happening, went off in hot pursuit of his beloved master, barking and whining like a dog gone crazy.

"Oh no," said Ben, bleary eyed and looked at his bedside clock - five fifteen in the morning. "Look Dad, just what I

always wanted," exclaimed Jack.

Jess rubbed her eyes and sat up. "Do get off the bed, Montgomery," she said. Jack plonked the electric train set on his parents' bed. "That's really wonderful, son," said Ben.

"Can we set it up now, Dad?" said Jack.

"How about we all get up and have breakfast first?" said Jess, getting out of bed. "Oh, isn't it cold?"

Celia popped her head around the bedroom door. "Come on. The fire is well alight in the big sitting room, and the kettle is on."

The family piled into the warm room. After the children had gone to bed the previous evening, hectic activity by the grown-ups had resulted in parcels of varying sizes being piled under the enormous Christmas tree. Alice was quiet. Then she went over to her mum, threw her arms around her and said, " Thanks, Mum" and did the same to her dad. She had been given riding lessons at Blueberry Stables, a riding hat, crop and boots. It was a dream come true. Now she would be able to go riding with her friend Jilly Mathers. So her mum and dad had been aware of her desire to learn horse riding after all. Well how could they not know? She hardly ever stopped talking horses.

The family enthused about their Christmas presents. The Rupert Annual was well received by Alice, who loved the little bear. The train set was a big hit for Jack, as were all the other gifts, including knitted scarves and gloves, selection boxes, perfume and socks for the grown-ups, a compendium of games for Alice and Jack to share - in fact a cornucopia of plenty.

It was now about seven thirty on Christmas morning and from the kitchen were the beautiful aromas of freshly ground coffee and bacon. "How many eggs would you like, Ben?" asked Jess. She and Celia were on breakfast duties; it was a case of having to be, as Ben, Alex and the children were seated on the sitting room floor surrounded by train tracks. A train set comprising a handsome shiny green and brown engine, goods wagons, in fact, all the paraphernalia that went into a train set, was there.

"No, Dad, it doesn't go there," said Jack, becoming agitated with his dad and Alex. "I can do it."

Celia came to call them all for breakfast to find both men sat cross-legged in the middle of the train track and young Jack looking perplexed. "Tell them, Gran," he pleaded.

Celia smiled to herself and said, "I was beginning to wonder who Santa Claus brought the train set for. Come on, or breakfast will be cold."

As they all tucked into the tasty meal, there was a knock at the side door. "Come in," said Ben, "the door's open." Barnaby poked his head round.

"Could Alice and Jack step outside for a moment?" he said. "We had a delivery last night but I'm sure it came to the wrong house." Jack scrambled outside and stopped dead in his tracks. Alice was close behind him. There on the snow were two impressive-looking sledges; one bright blue in colour, the other dark red.

"Wow!" said Jack. "Are they for us?"

"I can't see me or Nora on 'em, can you?" said Barnaby.

"Oh, Dad, can we go down to the bottom field?" asked Jack.

Ben shook the hand of this man who gave so much of himself to this family. He'd been aware for some time now that the gardener had been busy in the shed making something, but he didn't expect work of such a high standard. The sledges were magnificent, even down to the steel runners.

"Yes, Jack, we'll all go after we have been to the Carol Service this morning. The Reverend Jefferies is expecting us. Now have you two finished your breakfast? If so go and get ready. The service starts at ten and we don't want to be late, especially as Alex is singing a solo."

As the family arrived at St Peter's the sky had turned grey again, but it didn't feel quite as cold. "It looks like snow again," said Celia.

"How can you tell, Gran?" asked Jack.

"Oh, you just get used to the signs, love," she answered. Jack thought his gran was very wise. He gave her that special look and Celia gave her grandson a hug. "Now come on," she said. "We'd better find a seat."

The carol service began with a Nativity Play by the little children of Tiny Tots Nursery in the village; then a few carols before the Rev Paul Jefferies gave a short sermon on the birth of baby Jesus on that very special day 2000 years ago. Then Alex sang his solo, a beautiful rendition of 'O, Little Town of Bethlehem'. The rich baritone voice touched many in the church and there were murmurs of "Oh, what a lovely voice," heard echoing around the congregation.

Celia felt a swell of pride for this man who had found his way into her heart. As they left the church a carpet of fresh snow lay on top of the hard-packed snow that had fallen earlier.

"It's all new again!" said Jack, picking up a handful. "It will make our sledging a lot better, won't it, Dad?"

Ben shook hands with the Rev. Paul Jeffries, commenting that it was a very nice service. "Nice to see you all again," said the Reverend.

Then Ben said, "Come on then, you lot. Let's get home and have a warm drink before we go for a toboggan ride down the bottom field." With that Jack gave a loud whoopee. His dad was brilliant! So they all piled into the car and they were off.

"Gran and I will come down to watch you for a while, then we must go and prepare our Christmas lunch," said Jess as the family and Alex trudged to the top of the field, Alice and Jack pulling their sledges.

After about half a dozen rides down the hill, the walk back became harder and harder and Ben, sensing the fatigue in both his children said, "I'm ready for my lunch. Are we all ready?"

Alex cupped his hands together and blew into them saying, "I'm looking forward to mine. All this fresh, frosty air has given me an appetite."

"Come on then," said Ben, "back to the Grange."

As they approached the side door, the beautiful aroma met them. "Roast goose and veg," said Jack to his sister. "I do hope mum has done roast potatoes as well."

"Of course she has, Jack. It's Christmas," said his sister. "It will be a banquet."

The sledging party removed their wet boots at the door. "Come and get your slippers on," said Gran, who was waiting for them. "You're just in time. How about you, Alex? Did you bring slippers?" Alex said they were in his room and Jack offered to bring them, before they all sat down to their meal. Everyone agreed that the meal was delicious. Crackers were pulled, and stories were told, especially by the older generation, about what Christmases used to be like when they were young. Alice and Jack enjoyed tales about the old days, and Alice asked what Christmas was like when the Grange was built.

Ben remarked that since it was about four hundred years ago, it would have been very different to Christmas now. "Would you have liked to have been here then, Dad?"

"I don't really know, love. I would have had to wear breeches and a silly hat and the men in those days wore powdered wigs."

Jack laughed. "You would look really daft, Dad. Mum and Gran would have looked nice though. The ladies of that day wore really beautiful dresses. It was supposed to be a very romantic time: swashbuckling pirates, intrigue, excitement, danger."

Alice and Jack continued to ask questions about the old days and Christmas Day passed happily, with party games and lots to eat and drink. Jack was sick and so was Montgomery. "Hasn't it been a lovely day though?" said Jack, when he'd quite recovered from throwing up all over the sitting room floor.

The children had been tucked up in bed after the busy day, and Jess, Ben and Alex were reflecting on the excellent day over a sherry. "I think it has been my best Christmas day for many a long year," said Ben. "My mind is settled after such a long time of wondering what the sad history of my family was all about, and I do hope and pray that somehow my mum and dad have found peace at last."

Jess took her husband's hand, for she had always been acutely aware of the pain deep within him. "Everything will be fine from now on, love. You'll see. How do the rest of you feel about having a grand party for the re-naming of the Grange on New Year's Day - back to Bristow Grange?"

"What an excellent idea," said Ben, and the rest of them were all in favour. "We can invite Paul Jeffries and the historians who found out so much about the history of this old house."

"Do you think we have time to send invitations?" said Celia.

"Yes, if we start now," said Ben. So that being decided they all retired for the night. Boxing Day found them devising the best way to invite their guests at such short notice.

"We can ring most of them, and the few I know who aren't on the phone, I can pay a visit," said Alex by way of a thank you, for he really had been made to feel part of everything.

"Wow, another party!" said Alice and Jack, excited. "Can we ask our friends?"

"Why not?" said Ben. "The more the merrier." And from then on until New Year's Day the Grange was a hive of feverish activity.

"We'll have to use this large sitting room," said Jess to her mum.

"I just hope the long table will be all right, but as we decided on a buffet it will be ideal for the spread. I'm sure people would much rather have an informal get together. The decorations from Christmas and the fairy lights will look lovely along with balloons and poppers that the children insisted we must have."

"How many people do you think will come, Gran?" said Alice who'd just come in from the garden, where she and Jack were having a snowman competition.

"About thirty, if they all come," Celia replied.

"Where's Dad? We want him to come and judge who has made the best snowman" said Jack.

"I think you will find him with Barnaby. We would like Nora and him to come to the party," said his gran.

When he returned Ben asked Jess to help him with the difficult task of choosing the best snowman. "We just can't choose," he said at length, after looking the two snowmen over. "They are both equally good. Jack's has the best nose, but Alice's has the best hat; so we all agree that they are both the best. Now I'm feeling cold, so I suggest that we all go indoors and have a warming drink."

CHAPTER TEN
The Grand Re-naming back to Bristow Grange

The party was going with a swing. Twenty eight people had managed to make it, despite the weather taking a turn for the worse. Blizzard conditions had been forecast for the next few days and it was blowing a gale outside with driving snow. But inside the Grange everyone was enjoying the festivities. Alex was standing by the huge fireplace and said, "Can I have everyone's attention, please? Can I ask everyone to raise their glasses and toast Ben, Celia and the children at this the re-naming of their home back to its original name "Bristow Grange"? God bless this lovely home and all who live here."

The fire blazed in the hearth, glasses were raised, and everyone wished the new family well in their beautiful re-named "Bristow Grange". The party carried on well into the early hours, the families with young children having said their goodbyes around nine p.m. Alice and Jack went to bed about the same time, having thoroughly enjoyed the evening. The Grange was still full of a lovely atmosphere with people sitting around chatting to each other, and food and drink were plentiful. Soft music played on the gramophone and a few couples were dancing.

Ben held his wife as they attempted a waltz. "I'm no good at this, love," he said with a shy smile. Jess gave him a peck on the cheek. "You're doing just fine" she replied, and they gazed with happiness into each other's eyes.
"Look at Mum and Alex," said Jess.

"I know, Jess. Isn't it wonderful?" said Ben. "I think they were made for each other."

Celia was looking radiant and Alex looked to be on cloud nine. They danced close in each other's arms, oblivious to anyone else in the room, or to anyone else on the planet.

Ben called out, "Just look at that snow! And the wind is whipping up a real storm out at sea. I'm going upstairs to take a look from our room. It gives a wonderful view of the ocean. Come with me if you like, but please be quiet. I don't want to disturb the children."

Alex and a couple of the guests followed Ben. "Where else could you witness such power?" he said. "Just look at those mighty waves. In the time we have lived at the Grange, we have never experienced anything like this."

As the waves crashed against the cliffs the sound was deafening. "Isn't it awesome?" said one of the guests. "I'm rather glad we are in here and not down there."

Ben had been thinking since the storm had been getting more ferocious during the party that it might be an idea to ask the guests if any of them would like spend the night at the Grange, hoping conditions for travelling would improve by tomorrow. "Well," remarked Jess to Ben, "We do have the room. We may not have enough beds for everyone, but we do have sleeping bags." So it was decided and most guests opted to stay, while the remaining few said they would risk the journey home, and so the party night came to an end with the guests who had decided to stay sorting out where they would all sleep with much giggling and fun due to the drink they had imbibed during the evening.

Ben stood at the door waving off friends who were going home. "If you can't make it, come back and we will fix you up for the night," he said to each guest. Goodbyes were said and Ben was happy to close the door on the storm. He put an arm around his wife, saying, "My, but it's rough out there, love. I'm glad we're not travelling in it. Come on; let's see if everyone is settled. Then it's off to bed for us."

Morning came bright and calm after the horrendous night of battling winter weather. The next day they could hardly believe it was the same ocean, as Ben and Jess stood looking out on quite a different scene. The gentle waves lapped and caressed the shore, and gone were the angry, foaming Leviathans crashing their anger onto granite cliffs. Snow still covered the beach, dirty and covered in flotsam and jetsam now, for gone was the innocent untouched fall of the previous day.

Once again a solitary seagull cried his lonesome song to the sky. "I think he's our own special seagull," said Jess. "I like to think so, anyway."

Ben loved his gentle Jess. She could be right. Perhaps he was their own good luck emblem, and now that the house had been renamed Bristow Grange, as it had been all those years ago back in 1570, when it was first built by Benjamin Charles Bristow, perhaps the old Grange would stop the sighing sounds of sadness that could be detected on certain occasions. "Now then, has everyone had enough breakfast?" said Celia standing at the dining room door, check pinafore over her dressing gown. The guests who had decided to stay the night had tucked into a hearty hot breakfast, and the aroma of bacon and eggs wafted around the house, mingled with coffee that gently percolating, tempting guests to enjoy another cup. A chorus of "That was lovely!" came from satisfied friends who had found the whole experience very enjoyable. So with goodbyes all round, and thanks expressed from all the guests, people got into their cars and drove down the long drive back to their respective homes.

Ben and the family waved their friends goodbye and went into the house, Celia heaving a sigh of relief. "I'm pleased it went well, but I will be glad of a rest." Ben put a comforting arm around his mum-in-law.

"You and Jess have done a wonderful job," he said. "All our guests had five-star treatment."

"Oh, go on with you," said Celia, "but I could do with a nice cup of tea," and as they sat enjoying the peace and quiet, Jack came into the kitchen.

"It's snowing again - big flakes, and it's getting windy," he said.

Ben went to the door, exclaiming. "My goodness! I hope everyone got home all right! Just look at it, blizzard conditions again." This continued for the next few days. Snow piled up all over the orchard and garden, and delivery men found difficulty plying their wares to people's homes.

Ben and Barnaby tried their best to keep the drive clear of snow, and Fred the butcher managed to get through, saying, "By gum, I didn't think I would make it, but I thought I'd better bring extra meat."

"Thank you so much," said a relieved Jess. "I see you've brought mince. Good, for I think a cottage pie will go down a treat tomorrow with the children."

"Oh aye, it seems to be a favourite with kiddies. My two are partial to it an' all," said Fred, and with that Fred was on his way.

"I wanted to go sledging this morning," said a disgruntled Jack. "Look at that lovely deep snow over the bottom field."

"The trouble is, Jack," said Ben, "the snow has drifted so much, that it would be almost impossible to reach the bottom field."

"But, Dad, I'm fed up and so is Alice. Mum and Gran are writing letters, so they don't want us in the way."

"Why don't you both go upstairs and look at the waves crashing on the rocks?" said their father.

"We've just been doing that," said Jack. Just then Jess, hearing her disgruntled son, came into the room.

"I have an idea," she said. "Why don't you both go down in the cellar and see what you can find to do? I noticed various boxes stacked against the walls. It might be fun. The weather really isn't fit to be out in, Jack. You can go on your sledge just as soon as it clears up."

"OK," said Jack, " I'll ask Alice if she wants to go into the cellar," and with that Jack hurried off to find his sister.

"What do we want to go down there for?" said Alice.

"Oh, come on. You never know, it might be fun," her brother replied. Jack had cheered up with the prospect of delving into boxes, wondering what they might find.

Alice had a thought. They had lived at the Grange for a few months now and they had never been in the cellar, so they walked towards the low door along the passage. It was situated alongside what used to be the boot room, which their dad had told them was used to keep the tack in when the Grange had horses.

"I wish I had a horse of my own," said Alice to her brother.

"You will one day, Alice," he said. "We've already got stables." They opened the creaky cellar door. Hetty, who was always curious, had followed the children, and in a flash she was inside the door.

"Quick, put the light on," said Jack, looking to the side of the opening. He could see a switch, and as he turned on the dim light, they saw the back end of Hetty disappearing behind a large wooden box that was on the opposite side of the cellar.

"Hetty, Hetty, come back here!" Alice screamed at Jack. "Where's she gone?"

Jack reached the large trunk first and got down on his knees and peered into a tiny hole. "How did she get in there? Quick, let's see if we can move the box out of the way," he said. So using all their strength the two pulled and puffed with all their might. The heavy wooden object moved a little, so the pair rested a while and tried again. This time they had cleared about eighteen inches.

"I can hear her meowing. She's frightened. We must get in there," said Alice, starting to panic. "Go and fetch Dad, Jack, while I stay with Hetty."

Ben, Celia and Jess came running into the cellar. "What's going on?" Alice in garbled English tried to explain that Hetty had disappeared behind the wall. Then Ben took control. "Don't worry, love, I'll get her out," and with one heave the large wooden trunk was moved to one side. "Would you believe it?" A low archway had been concealed behind the trunk, bricked up for years, and Hetty had found a small hole where the plaster or brick had rotted away.

Ben got down on his hunkers and shone his torch into the hole. "Well, just look at that," he gasped.

"What is it, Dad?" asked Jack. In the shaft of torchlight Ben could see a passage leading downwards. The family took a look in turn. "I wonder where it leads to," said young Jack, boredom completely gone. Ben pulled at a few loose bricks which came away quite easily. "Can I go in, Dad?" asked Jack, beside himself with excitement.

"No, son. It may not be safe. I'll go and fetch my hammer. You can carry on calling to Hetty, though. See if she'll come out of there." So while Ben was away, the family called and called and eventually a wide-eyed cat crawled out of the hole, much to the delight of a very anxious Alice.

"Come here, you silly puss," said the very relieved girl, picking up the frightened cat. Hetty did what she always did when frightened. She stuck her head into the crook of her mistress's arm as if to say, "I'm safe. Just let me stay here for a while." Alice hugged her pet saying, "You're all right now," and with that Alice took Hetty back into the kitchen and gave her a drink of milk, before meeting her Dad coming back to the cellar.

"Oh good, you've got her" said Ben, relieved, for he was fond of the big lump, as he called Hetty. Once back in the cellar with the tools he needed to smash through the wall, he told the waiting family that he'd decided to give Alex a ring. "I know he hasn't been home very long after his visit with us, but being the historian that he is, I was sure he would be interested. Well, he was delighted, and will be here shortly."

Celia couldn't conceal her joy that Alex was coming back. She knew by now that he was the one for her. When Ben went back down into the cellar he told Jack to shine the torch onto the hole. Ben had managed to enlarge the opening using the big lump hammer. "Can you hear that loud sighing sound? That's the noise we can hear at different times," said Celia. "It's much louder now and seems to be coming from down there."

"Perhaps it's a ghost," said Jack.

"Oh shut up, you," said Alice, who'd just come back after settling Hetty. She didn't like talking about ghosts. "There are no such things so stop that, Jack."

"Don't frighten your sister," said Ben. "Just concentrate on what you're supposed to be doing." Then he carried on knocking down as much stone and brick as he could. The cellar was by now becoming rather dusty, and Jess left for a while, returning with scarves, giving one to each member of the family.

"Cover your mouths. We don't want brick dust in our throats," she said.

"Good idea, love," said Ben, wrapping a scarf around his face.

"You look like Billy the Kid, Dad," said Jack.

"I think we will be able to get through now," said Ben as he shone his torch into the blackness. "We could do with more light," he said "so pass me your torch, Jack." The lad did as he was asked and his father said, "There's a man made path here! Looks like it's been hewn out of solid rock!" Ben climbed onto a narrow path that sloped down between black damp walls, which gave off a musty pungent smell.

Ben said he was going down a little way and Jess told him to be careful as she was worried for her hubby. "Why don't you wait for Alex?" she asked.

"Don't worry. I won't go far," he replied.

Ben was able to walk upright though the floor was a bit slippery, but if he walked by the wall he could steady himself. He felt himself to be gradually going down, but wasn't it dark and the smell was horrible. He felt a sort of ancient foreboding, and now and again he felt something touch his face like cobwebs. "Spiders can get simply anywhere," he told himself.

Then he heard Jess cry, "Ben, Ben, Alex has just arrived. Come back, love."

"OK, I'm coming," replied Ben turning around gingerly, but there wasn't much room to do that easily. He climbed out into the cellar and the friends shook hands.

"Look at the cobwebs, Dad. Your hair is covered in them," said Jack.

Alex smiled. "My goodness, some of them have been down there a long time. What was it like?"

"Awesome, and a bit scary to be honest. I only went a short way, but it was obvious to me that the tunnel or path went much further down; but because the torches gave only very limited light, I found it difficult to be accurate."

"Right then," said Alex. "Let's try this halogen light."

Alex passed it to Ben, who said, "Come on then" and Alex followed his friend through the large hole and into the passageway. The stronger light showed much more detail. Ben pointed it upwards and the ceiling of the tunnel was sort of arched. From floor to ceiling the pair estimated the height to be six feet.

"You're right about the pong," said Alex, screwing his nose up. "How far do you reckon this goes?"
"I don't know, Alex."
"Then come on. Let's find out" said Ben, and the two men inched their way steadily downwards, the strong light being a big help.
"Look, Ben, that green stuff on the walls looks like algae; and it feels slimy," said Alex as they walked steadily onwards and downwards. They encountered cobwebs all the way, and every now and again they heard that weird sighing sound that they had been aware of ever since moving into the Grange.
As they carried on further, so the noise became louder; then just as soon it stopped again and Ben remarked that he hoped they'd soon find out what it was. They didn't have long to wait. When they'd travelled about one hundred yards, they were stopped by what looked like a rock fall. Ben shone the strong light onto the giant pile and exclaimed, "My goodness! I wonder what happened here. In fact, to tell you the truth, Alex, I'm wondering about the whole lot."
As Ben spoke a deafening howl penetrated the tunnel. "What the heck was that? It sounded like a hurricane," said Ben, continuing to shine the halogen light towards the rock fall.
Alex said, "Ben, I felt a gust of wind on my face" and lifting his arm up in the direction of where it came from, his hand detected a hole as big as an orange located towards the top of the rock fall. "There's a strong wind coming through here, Ben, and I suppose the hole being

so small accounts for the noise it makes, forcing its way through."

"You could be right. I know a lady who will be very relieved when we tell her that the source of all the sighing and howling has been discovered." Ben had to admit that he found the noises a bit off putting, but he would never have let on to Jess or Celia. In fact he had always made light of it when the children asked about the sighing, telling them it was the sound of the house sleeping!

On further investigation of the rock fall, the two men decided that it was going to be a mammoth task to clear all the rocks. Just how they were going to tackle the job would take a great deal of planning. "How about we go and tell the others what we have found?" said Ben. "Then together we may be able to formulate a plan." So with that the friends made their way back to the cellar.

CHAPTER ELEVEN
The Big Dig

"Well, would you believe it?" Celia was the first to speak after hearing about what the two men had discovered beyond the hole in the cellar. "A pathway you say, and a rock fall. How very exciting, and what a relief to know at long last just where the noises are coming from. I will sleep much easier in my bed from now on."

"How long do you think the tunnel has been there, Dad?" said Alice.

"It's hard to say, Alice, but many years, I would say. Now we have to devise a plan for shifting the rocks."

"Can't you just bash them down, Dad?"

"No, son. We need a strategy to work to. The whole tunnel will need shoring up."

"What do you mean, Dad?"

"We'll need timber like they use down the coal mines, and remember that film we saw on the telly the other day about British prisoners during the war, 'The Great Escape', how they dug a secret tunnel out of the prison camp?"

"Yes, Dad. It was good."

"Well, Jack, they used lots of wood to strengthen the sides of the tunnel as they went along. We must do something on similar lines."

"Ooh! Can we pretend to be prisoners and we're digging ourselves out? I won't take Montgomery down the tunnel though, cos he would be too scared."

"Just hang on, son. It will be very dangerous down there, and in any case it will be quite a time before we start taking wood down. We have to make the opening at the cellar end much bigger, then we must try to do something about the slippery floor."

"How about scattering sand?" said Jess.

"Good idea, love. It's treacherous walking down the path. We would never carry planks of timber."

"But I want to help, Dad," said Jack.

"I know you do, and you will. Just try to have a little patience, Jack, there's a good lad."

Later, the grown ups sat around the kitchen table, drinking a cup of tea. "We will need lots of timber, nails and screws, and at least three large buckets, and we could do with another Halogen light as well." It was decided that the men would measure the part of the tunnel to be shored up, then they could order the timber required.

A few days later everything was in place. The wood arrived on an articulated lorry. "I'm glad it's Saturday and I'm not at school," said a very excited Jack. "When are you going to start?"

"Don't be in such a rush," said his father. "Why don't you take Montgomery for his walk while we unload? Because when we start later on we are going to need your help."

Alice was much more interested in her pony class, so Celia had taken her to the stables earlier that morning knowing full well what the topic of conversation would be. "When do you think Dad will buy me my own pony?" Celia had answered this question a dozen times or more. "I don't know, dear. I think Mum and Dad would like you to have more lessons before they decide."

"But I can ride all right now, Gran," said Alice.

"Just try to be a little patient. I feel sure it won't be too long. You know that your dad and Alex are very busy at the moment." Alice looked downcast, so Celia said,

"Don't worry, darling," and gave her grand-daughter a hug. "Just wait a while and you'll get your pony soon."

Meanwhile, Ben and Alex started to assemble the wood and all the other paraphernalia needed to shore up the tunnel. They carried it bit by bit to the cellar, and had moved the wooden box out of the way to give them easier access through the hole. So with two mighty halogen torches they stepped back into the opening.

"Have you got the tape measure, Ben?"

"Yes, and I brought some string. You never know, it may come in useful. We could fasten one end at the entrance and use it as a guide in case we get lost."

Alex smiled at his friend. "Ha, ha very funny," he quipped.

Jess was at the entrance of the tunnel. It was to be her job to help pass equipment to the men once they were through. Barnaby had been roped in to help and had gone ahead, waiting at the sight of the fall. Plank by plank the wood was passed down the narrow tunnel. Each piece had been measured and cut to size, but only when the first few had been put into place could the men attempt to start knocking through, but through... to what? Nobody knew and it was not surprising really, because after extensive investigation by the Historical Society nothing had been found relating to the secret tunnel. Nobody knew of its existence until Hetty was seen disappearing behind the big wooden box.

"I think it's very mysterious to think that after all these years and the different people who have lived at the Grange that it had to be our Hetty who discovered the way into the tunnel." Celia was talking to Jess. She and Alice had just returned home from the stables. "I've known from the first day that Bristow Grange held a sort of magic. So it follows that we had to be the ones to uncover all the hidden secrets. Willerby Grange was waiting for the return of the Bristow family to regain her rightful name."

"I agree with you, Mum," said Jess. "For as you know I've always loved old buildings, and firmly believe that the walls soak up the characters of the people who lived there; and in the case of the old Grange, she just waited her time."

"Oh, Jess, how romantic, love!" Celia had always been aware of this trait in her daughter's make-up. She had always been deep feeling and gentle. Her dad used to say she was a dreamer, but Celia knew her daughter was special.

Alex appeared at the opening of the tunnel and said, "A few more barrow loads and we are through." He manoeuvred the wheelbarrow into the cellar, looked round and said, "My goodness! We've got quite a pile already, but it will have to stay there until the snow clears and we can move the rocks and rubble outside."

Jack came over from the rock pile and asked when he could go down the tunnel. "We need to move the rest of the rubble," said his dad, "then you can go and have a look. You've done an excellent job, Jack." Ben had just appeared at the entrance with another wheelbarrow-ful.

"Come on," said Celia, "time for a break. The coffee pot is on and I've made some sandwiches. You both look like miners. Give Barnaby a shout, will you? He must be ready for a drink."

"Do I look like a miner, Mum?" said Jack, looking at Jess.

"Considering that you have been stacking the rocks against the cellar wall as your dad and Alex have brought them along the passage, I think you look every bit a miner." Jack beamed. He so wanted to emulate his dad. Ben had always been the lad's hero.

"This coffee is going down a treat. I was beginning to feel parched," said Alex as he drank deeply of the nectar. "You make a good cup." He looked shyly at his love and Celia felt a flush on her cheeks.

She nudged his arm. "Go on with you," she said, and the rest of the group smiled. Those two really had feelings for each other. "How much longer before you break through the rock fall?" said Celia, trying to get back to the matter in hand.

"Not long now. If we carry on at this pace we will have the lot down by tomorrow lunch time. It's almost four thirty. How about we call it a day?" The men looked at each other, and it was decided to take Celia's advice. Alex had been asked by Ben to stay the night so they could get an early start.

Of course Alex accepted because the invitation was a twofold pleasure. He would be able to spend more time with Celia, and he was so intrigued by the adventure unfolding before them. This old house was about to give up a secret, and he wanted to be in on it.

CHAPTER TWELVE
Through to the Other Side

"Ladies, that sure was a lovely meal. It's a long time since I tasted beef as tender as that: and the Yorkshire pudding, I could swear I have never enjoyed better." Alex sat back in his chair and thought to himself how fortunate he was. Fate had led him to these dear people at a time in his life when he seemed to be only looking on and never taking part in anything to do with real life; merely going through the motions.

Friends had done their best over the years since he had become a widower and the Historical Society was a real source of interest, but he still couldn't get used to going home to an empty house. The lonely evenings and nights were the hardest to take. It was the quiet; nobody to enquire about the day, but how different was his life now. Fate had seen fit to shine on him. These lovely people were to be his future.

He hadn't stopped pinching himself yet, but it wasn't a dream. It was real, and he had found his new love along with a wonderful family. He awoke in the morning, refreshed from a peaceful night's sleep. He bathed and the aroma of bacon from the kitchen led him there to find the family tucking in.

"Ah, there you are, Alex. I was just coming to find you," said Ben.

"Sorry if I overslept folks, but once my head hit the pillow, I was away."

Celia smiled. "I'm glad you had a good night's sleep, love. You worked hard yesterday; in fact, you all did," she said.

Ben settled himself again and said, "I thought I would have to wake you, but no, you must have smelt the fry-up." Jess passed a plate of food to Alex.

"When can we start, Dad?" It was Jack, eager as ever to get on with the job.

"Just as soon as we have had breakfast, son; and we will need you to carry on doing the job you did yesterday," said his father.

"Can I go down the tunnel today, Dad?"

"It all depends. There's still quite a lot of rock to move, but we are hoping to be through to the other side shortly," and with that the gang made their way to the cellar to start the day's dig.

Barnaby arrived brushing the snow from his clothes. "By heck, will it ever stop snowing?" he said.

"Morning, Barnaby," said the diggers.

"We are certainly having a hard winter," said Alex, "that's for sure, but come on, let's get cracking."

Bucket after bucket was hauled up into the cellar to a waiting Jack, then the men swapped places: two knocking out, demolishing the pile, one putting the rocks into buckets then a wheelbarrow and transporting them to the lad.

Ben had just given another hefty swipe with his hammer when there was a loud rumble coming from the other side of the pile, with a mighty sounding crash. What sounded like a small avalanche could be heard tumbling away from the other side of the fall. The men listened with baited breath and after what seemed an age, but in reality was only seconds, the rumbling stopped. Then deathly quiet, and from the very top of the rock pile there came a loud sort of creaking sound. One enormous boulder came crashing down, missing the men by inches.

From the cellar came cries of, "Are you all right down there?"

"Yes, don't worry," said Ben, who was looking at an incredible scene, for the giant rock that had missed them by an inch had opened up a hole about three yards by two.

"Will you just look at that?" said Barnaby, who had managed to regain his composure. The three men were looking into the continuation of the tunnel.

"It's lighter that side," said Ben, as they gazed in awe at what they had uncovered. They could see that the tunnel seemed to veer slightly to the right. "How long do you reckon it is?"

Alex answered, "From what we can see, Ben, I would estimate roughly about the same as this side of the fall, and I suggest before we go any further we get more wood down here, and start to make safe the rest of the tunnel."

The other two men agreed, and as they all sat enjoying a cup of tea the talk was all about what had been uncovered. "Can I go down and look, Dad, please?" asked Jack.

"And me?" said his sister.

"Not at the moment, for as we have been saying, we need to make the tunnel much safer. The vibrations from the hammering we have been giving the rock fall must have loosened more of the stuff."

"But, Dad, when can we go down?" persisted Jack.

"I have told you, son, when we feel it's quite safe."

Jack pulled a petulant face and said, "I'm fed up of waiting."

Jess put an arm around Jack. "I know it's frustrating, love, but your dad is right. It will be worth the wait."

Jack sloped off, hands in his pocket saying, "It's not fair."

"Come on then, Alex," said Ben. "Let's get cracking."

Barnaby was already down at the rock pile, and the two friends could hear hammering on rock as they entered the cellar. Single file they walked down the now familiar path. The extra light coming through the large gap enabled them to see more clearly how long would it be before they could go through to the other side, and then what?

This sure was the adventure of a lifetime! These were Ben's thoughts as the two men picked their way down this pathway to goodness knew where. Eventually the wooden planks were all in place. "That's a pretty neat job even if I say it myself," said Alex.

"I agree, Alex, but I think it's time we called it a day. We have been down here for about three hours, and the ladies did say dinner would be ready at six pm. I don't know about you, but I am really looking forward to roast chicken with all the trimmings. Celia excels at sage and onion stuffing."

As they sat down to this lovely meal the talk was all about the tunnel and what might be beyond the rock fall and where the path would lead to. The grown-ups were so engrossed in the conversation that nobody saw Jack leave the table. "Come on, Montgomery," he said and the boy and dog entered the cellar. Jack knew he was doing wrong, but he must see for himself what the tunnel looked like and investigate the rock fall.

It was dark and he was a bit scared, but Montgomery was with him and he was going to be the pit pony. Jack had learned at school all about mining in the olden days, when ponies were used down the pits and it was dark for them. So he and Montgomery would be fine.

Jack had brought the torch that his gran had bought him when they first arrived in Yorkshire, and the strong beam of light shone down the pathway. Montgomery went ahead, sniffing the new smells with interest, but Jack, realising that the path was quite slippery, walked very slowly.

Eventually he arrived at the rock fall. Montgomery being able to smell the air coming into the tunnel through the large hole put his two front legs onto the pile of rocks. "You can't get up there, Montgomery. Let me try," said Jack, and with that he started to climb.

He managed to reach the gap with his fingers as he lifted himself up to take a look through the large hole, and, with a shout of, "I can see a bright light!" Jack missed his footing and started to slip. He banged his chin on the rocks as he careered downwards, crashing to the ground with a loud thud. Then he lay motionless.

Montgomery, sensing his master was in trouble, proceeded to lick Jack's face, but the lad remained still; so Montgomery did the only thing he could do, bark as loud as his voice would let him. He barked and he barked but to no avail, so after what seemed an age in dog time, he very reluctantly left his beloved master and traversed back up the tunnel again, barking as loud as his lungs would let him.

As he reached the cellar, Ben and the others, hearing the commotion, arrived in a panic. "What is it, boy? Where's Jack?" they asked.

The dog turned tail and ran back into the tunnel, closely followed by a very worried Ben. "I'm coming," said Jess.

"No, love. Stay here," said Ben.

Alex touched Celia's arm as he went past her and Jess said again, "Let us go, please." But with that both men and dog disappeared into the tunnel. What would they find?

"Dear God, please let him be all right," said Jess

"Jack! Jack! We're coming, son," said Ben, and the two men found Jack lying at the bottom of the rock pile.

Ben felt for a pulse. "Thank God, he's alive. I'll go and tell the ladies and ring for the doctor," said Alex.

"Thanks, Alex," said Ben.

Jack was taken into hospital as a precaution, for he suffered slight concussion and sported many bruises. When the panic was over Jess smiled with tears of relief when one of the nurses told them about the napkin containing a piece of chicken and two roast potatoes found in Jack's pocket when he was admitted.

The lad stayed in hospital for a few days, and when he came home and after a good talking to by his dad, he promised never to do anything like that again. But he told his dad, "It was exciting when I was up on the rock pile, for I saw a bright light coming through that hole. What was it, Dad?"

"I don't know, son. We haven't been down since you fell," said Ben.

Eventually normality returned and work continued on the rock pile, which was significantly reduced after Jack's fall, for as he tumbled he brought quite a bit with him. The men carried on shoring up as they went and eventually the pile was cleared. "Shall we ask the rest of the family to come down?" said Alex. "Then we can all discover together where the tunnel leads."

"Good idea," said Ben, so it was decided that the next day was to be the big day, and after breakfast on this auspicious day, January 15th 1980, the family plus Alex, who was like family anyway, journeyed down the tunnel and out at the other end.

"It's the beach," said Jack. "But just look at the big boulder. It must be ten feet high by eight feet wide!"

Looming right in front of the tunnel opening around the bottom of the huge rock was a gorse bush, as if planted there on purpose; perhaps as extra disguise to conceal the newly discovered tunnel from the beach side.

Jack was the first out. "It's massive!" he cried. From the tunnel opening the boulder stood about six feet away. The excited lad stepped onto the sand and ran to the huge rock form, leaned against it and, spreading his arms out as if trying to measure the circumference, said, "Can I climb it, Dad?"

Ben looked at his son. "No you can't. We had enough trouble with your climbing the other day."

The rest of the family piled out of the tunnel. The cold nip in the air caught their breath. Snow had drifted up one side of the boulder and along the cliffs, and the beach itself was covered in what looked like waves of snow where the cruel wind had teased and whipped the flakes into submission. Seaweed and dirty sea froth lapped along the shore line, leaving a tide mark of brown stain in its wake. "I wonder how far those logs of wood have travelled," said Jess, intrigued.

"It's hard to say, love," said Ben. "Who feels like beachcombing?"

They all decided it would be a good idea, so even though it was bitterly cold they set off in the direction of the logs and they encountered lots of debris on the way.

"How does all this rubbish get here, Dad?" asked Jack.

"I don't really know, son. It could be that we are in a small bay and once it gets in on a high tide, it stays in."

"Don't forget," said Alex, "that the winter this year has been exceptionally bad."

They investigated the logs of wood that were scattered along the beach; some very large, others small.

"They could have come from anywhere," said Ben. "As Alex has told you, the weather this winter has been atrocious, whipping the sea up into terrible conditions not only on this stretch of coastline, but much further afield. It's always reckoned that if America encounters bad weather, then we will get it shortly afterwards. I don't know how true that is, but it seems to follow."

"Yes, I tend to agree with you, Ben," said Alex. "And I think it's time we went back home. My feet are frozen. What about you two?"

Celia looked at the children and Alice took her grandmother's hand, as the intrepid beachcombers headed for the path. "Can't we go back up the tunnel?" asked Jack.

"I think we'd better do a bit more shoring up first, son, just to be on the safe side," said his father. So they all headed for the path which was situated just left of the tunnel entrance. As they approached, Jess mentioned how strange it was that it was impossible to see the tunnel entrance from the beach.

"How odd. It's as if the boulder had been strategically placed there in order to conceal the entrance. But surely not. Who would do that? And why?"

CHAPTER THIRTEEN
Who Would Believe It?

They all sat enjoying a hot chocolate and discussed in detail all they had discovered. "What do you think all those hooks and peg things were, Dad, sticking out of the walls at the bottom of the tunnel? What did it mean? Who do you think put them there, Dad?"

"I don't know, Jack. It's a mystery and no mistake, but I believe this old house is full of all sorts of mystery, and one day all will be revealed."

"Will it be scary, Dad?"

Ben was answering his daughter now. She had been listening intently to her brother's questions and, to be honest, she didn't like the tunnel. It was too frightening for her. What if Hetty found her way to the tunnel? She would be so scared. No. She didn't like the tunnel at all. It wasn't for girls. She would do her best to make sure that Hetty didn't come anywhere near the passage, especially as the rock fall had been cleared, for it was now a straight run through to the beach. No. Alice didn't like it at all, for if Hetty got on to the beach she would be frightened.

Ben, Alex and Barnaby continued shoring the tunnel on both sides, only stopping temporarily when they reached the bend.

"I think this needs a bit more discussion," said Ben to the two men.

"It looks as if it's going to be difficult," Alex answered. He was wondering how they were going to overcome this obstacle when just then they heard, "Come on, you miners. Dinner is ready!"

It was Jess. Ben thought to himself they must have been down here for ages. "I don't know about you two," he said, "but I'm starving" and with that the men climbed the path and stepped into the cellar.

Barnaby said his goodbyes after declining the offer of a hot meal. "Right then, we'll see you in the morning, Barnaby, and thanks for your help."

With that Barnaby headed for the Coach House, and Nora's stew. "Come on, Dad. Look what Gran and Mum made for dinner.

"One of my favourites," said Ben, "chicken in the basket."

"Mine, too," said Alex. "Oh, you two get worse. Sit down and have your dinner," said Celia, and the two men did as they were asked. Celia smiled to herself. It was so wonderful that these two men had become such good pals in such a short time. It was true, the Grange had magical powers, and they all enjoyed an excellent meal. Treacle tart following the main course.

"Any more custard, Mum?"

"My goodness, where you manage to put it all is a mystery to me" said Jess, looking lovingly at her son. He could be a little monkey at times, but she had been aware, since their move to the Grange, just how much the lad had come out of his shell. No more the quiet shy Jack. The boy had really taken to life in this beautiful old house. "Would you like more tart to go with your custard, Jack?" she asked. Jack gave his mum the cheeky smile that always warmed her heart. Boys and men, they know just which strings to pull.

Alice meanwhile had finished her dinner and was talking to her gran about the fear she had of the tunnel. "I understand your fear, darling. The tunnel being opened up from the cellar to the beach is very frightening, but please don't worry any more. We were discussing the problem last night after you and Jack had gone to bed, and your dad and Alex have already got the problem in hand. Before the rest of the tunnel is shored up, wood is being delivered on Saturday morning so that the men can make a strong door for the cellar end of the tunnel. Barnaby is going to help your dad and Alex; so with the three of them on the job, the tunnel will be very secure."

Alice gave her gran a hug. "Oh Gran, what a relief!"

Celia understood why her granddaughter had been so worried, for even though the beach was private... you never knew.

Saturday morning arrived as Celia and Alice set off for the stables. The wood was being delivered and Ben said, "When you get back, we will be well on the way to having secure doors fitted."

"Bye, dad" said Alice giving her dad a kiss as she went happily to her horse riding class.

The wood was stacked in the cellar and the men rolled up their sleeves despite the weather being cold. The snow seemed to have stopped at last and it hadn't snowed for a few days, so everyone was hoping that they had seen the last of it; even Jack who had grown tired of making snow men. The slide had also lost its appeal, and he was looking for more challenging ways to spend his time.

"Come on then. Let's get started on these doors," said Ben.

It had been decided that because the bricks had been knocked out from under what looked like an original arch, they would make two security doors. "Why do you think the tunnel was built in the first place?" Jess had asked Ben.

"It seems the arch was made like that for easy access" he replied, "but for what reason, I just don't have a clue. What I can tell you is that the arch was probably built at the same time as the Grange - sort of built for a purpose."

"How fascinating," said Jess, intrigued. "So it was built for a purpose? And bricked up for a purpose? But it's strange nobody seems to know anything about the tunnel. There was nothing in the deeds. In fact there is nothing to indicate the tunnel being built at all. It's a mystery and no mistake. Well, I'll leave you men to it. Come up and have a cup of tea in a little while."

The men carried on sawing timber into shape, placing and hammering the pieces of wood until they had fashioned two secure doors. By the time the job was completed it was six thirty in the evening.

Alex took hold of the two sturdy handles on each door, and gave a tug. "Impenetrable," he said with a feeling of satisfaction, after they had previously locked and bolted the new doors. "You can all sleep safe in your beds now."

"Alice did you hear that, love?" said her grandmother.

"Yes. Thanks all of you," said Alice, when the men had finished the job and were all tucking into egg and chips and peas, Barnaby included, for Nora was out visiting a sick friend.

Everyone agreed that it was a job well done. Jack, though, was thinking along other lines. Last time they had all been down on the beach he had taken note of the logs of wood that were strewn along the bay. The family had investigated them with interest, but he had a vested interesting in them - goal posts. They would make splendid goal posts.

When friends had been to the Grange, he had thought to himself just what a wonderful football field the bottom large patch of grass would make; so when the logs had been discovered his mind conjured up a wonderful football pitch with the best goal posts, equal to Man United ground. Man United would be proud to play on Jack's ground. They could even have a friendly, The Grange against Man United.

After the meal was finished, Jack thought it a good idea to broach the subject. "It sounds OK to me," said Ben, feeling tired after a day of hard work. His arms ached after all the sawing, so he said, "Leave it until next Saturday. I have a few clients to see next week, and you have school."
Although a little disappointed his idea couldn't be achieved at once, Jack said, "Thanks, Dad," and went off to find Montgomery, to tell him of the plans for the following Saturday.

CHAPTER FOURTEEN
The Greatest Surprise of Them All

Saturday arrived at last. The weather was fine, and it seemed that the snow had finally said goodbye. It was still cold, but you could feel the subtle change: bit by bit mornings were getting lighter; the sea, that had been so angry, now, very gently, lapped the shore.

"Is Alex coming, Dad?" asked Jack.

"No. Not this morning. He will be here this evening though. It's just you and me. Alice and Gran are going to the stables as usual, and Mum is going to Axanbey shopping. Get your boots on, son. They will give better grip as we go down the tunnel."

Jack did as his dad asked and they headed for the cellar. "The doors look good, Dad," he said.

"Yes, son, and do you see that small hook on the wall to the side? Well, the key to these doors is to be kept there at all times. When you open the doors and shut the doors, always remember that."

"I will, Dad," he replied, and they set off with a torch each.

As they traversed down the long path, Jack thought to himself what a wonderful job his dad and the men had done on the tunnel. Both sides looked so neat and safe. "It's just like a real mine, Dad. Oh! I forgot Montgomery. Can I fetch him?"

"Go on then, for he loves the beach."

"Thanks, Dad" said Jack and boy and dog were soon back, Montgomery full of beans, tail wagging, tongue hanging out. Jack was happy that his best pal was sharing in the fun. The three intrepid adventurers reached the part of the tunnel where the rock fall had taken place, now devoid of rubble of any kind.

It was just below there that the path veered to one side.

"Look how light it is here, Dad."

"Do you remember what you told us about a light you saw just before your fall from the rock pile? It was night. So it was the moon, that bright light."

"Isn't this good, Dad? I love this place," said Jack. Soon they reached the beach and Montgomery bounded out onto the sand. There was not a trace of snow to be seen, though the remnants of a hard winter were all around, such as rubbish tossed up all over the sand.

Where did it come from? Which part of the world, and where had these logs originated? Father and son investigated each piece of drift wood in turn.

"I think we will be able to make two decent goal-posts," said Ben. "It looks like these logs have travelled for some time, judging by the state of them."

"They came to us like a present, Dad. They wanted to be goal-posts."

"Perhaps you're right," said his dad. "But we will never know. Mind you, so many wonderful things have been happening since we moved here that I am almost prepared to believe anything. Now come on, or we will never get started." With that, Ben took out his tape measure and proceeded to line up what he thought would be the most suitable logs for the job.

"We will only be able to take one at a time, for the largest ones are very heavy. Do you think you will be able to carry them, Jack?"

"I'll try, Dad."

"OK, you get to the front and we'll go a while, then have a rest. Then a little bit further, and so on." With that man and boy set off; however, after a few yards, Ben could see that Jack was struggling, but knowing his son Ben knew the lad wouldn't give in easily. Being diplomatic, father said to son "I don't know about you, Jack, but I think this is a three-man job."

So it was decided to wait until the next day when Alex would be available. He would be there that evening, staying overnight until Sunday evening. "Anyway, Dad, Alex wouldn't want to be left out, would he?"

So with Jack feeling relieved and feelings being spared, man and boy walked back towards the tunnel with Montgomery trailing behind. He would have stayed longer if he had been allowed, because it was lovely running along the soft sand and smelling all the lovely aromas, but his master was going home and he wasn't going to be left on his own. Anyway, the dog guessed it must be grub time as he'd seen the butcher deliver a box of interesting meat earlier. So it could be rabbit stew for him, his absolute favourite.

They arrived back home as Celia and Alice came into the drive. It was almost lunch time. "Who fancies Yorkshire fish and chips?" asked Celia. Jack realised how hungry he was, and fish and chips were his favourite. "Good job we brought them back with us then," Celia smiled.

As they sat enjoying the lovely meal straight out of the paper, they all agreed with Ben's comment, and they discussed how hard Ben and Jack had found the job of carrying the logs. Jack said, "So we decided to wait until Alex could help tomorrow."

"That's a splendid idea," said Celia, who knew Alex would be only too happy to help. Sunday morning arrived, weather calm, sky the palest blue, sea sort of quietly lapping the shore as if relieved to be free of the tempest that had reigned for so long, and a watery sun tried its best to warm the cold late winter morning. "It's not a bad day," said Alex.

Ben was relieved that his friend was giving a hand, for they would soon get the job done. It was decided that the largest logs were to be the first that were moved. Ben and Alex sorted through the wood, putting the largest by the entrance to the tunnel. "Now, Jack, if we carry the first big log, do you think you could carry a long thin one?"

Jack, feeling quite important, said yes, he could. With that the two men picked up the first heavy log, manoeuvred it through the entrance of the tunnel, stopped to rest, then proceeded yard by yard, puffing and panting until they reached the other end of the tunnel at the cellar side. Jack followed his dad, and Alex, his log being quite cumbersome, was finding the job more difficult than he thought, for as he came to the part of the tunnel that veered to one side the front of his log crashed with a thud into the opposite side of the wall, just below where the wooden supports came to an end; this part being delayed earlier so that the cellar end could be secured.

As Jack's log hit the wall, there was the sound of rocks falling, and the log seemed to penetrate with ease, and the two men came rushing back down the tunnel, worried at hearing the sound. A gaping hole appeared where the log of wood had disturbed the rock, and on careful investigation, Ben said, "It looks like another tunnel leading off this one."

The men shone their torches into the blackness, "Look!" said Alex transfixed, as the light from the torches had revealed a large oblong trunk!

"My goodness, how long has that been there? I don't think I like this. What the heck is it?" Ben sounded flabbergasted. "I'm going to see if I can get any closer."

"Be careful, Dad," said Jack.

"Don't worry" his father replied, and with that Ben stepped over the rubble to get closer to the trunk. "This is old. I mean really old."

He used his forearm to try to remove some of the muck and grime, and said, "It's made of a heavy sort of tin with wide bands coming over the lid. They look like brass, but it's hard to tell though; all I do know is that it's very old and I can't shift it. It's as solid as concrete. What's that at the front?"

Alex was shining his torch underneath what looked like the lid. "It's a massive keyhole," said Jack. "Look at the size of it!"

Alex managed to get alongside Ben and they tried to open the lid, but it was stuck fast. "No, we won't do it. It's locked," said Ben.

"Where do you think the key is, Dad? There must be one."

"I don't know. It's probably lost. We don't know how long this chest has been down here. Could be hundreds of years," said Ben.

"I know, Dad. Remember that big key you found in the big fireplace, which wouldn't fit any of the locks in the house? Perhaps it will fit the trunk," said Jack.

"That's brilliant, son," said his dad.

"I'll go and get it," said Jack, with that the excited lad made his way back up the tunnel and came back breathless with the massive key. "It fits! It fits!" he cried.

"Well, I'll be blowed " said his dad. "Clever lad. But it won't turn."

Both men tried unsuccessfully to turn the key, but it just wouldn't budge, and just then they heard Celia calling them for lunch. "Come on," said Ben. "I suggest we have our meal, and put some oil on the key."

So the key being well and truly soaked, every one sat down to enjoy a lovely hot pot. Whilst they sat around the table, naturally the talk was about what had been found in the tunnel. "A massive chest, you say?" said Jess, hardly able to take in yet another mystery surrounding the old Grange.

"How big is it, Dad?" said Alice, also intrigued. "Please can we go and see it?"

"I thought you were scared of the tunnel, Alice" said Ben.

"I don't like it, Dad, but a secret chest is so exciting, and I won't be on my own will I? Gran wants to see it as well."

"I'll tell you what, love," said her dad, "there isn't really room for all of us at once. So how about Alex and me go down with the key? And if we open the trunk, then we will come back and tell you what we find. Then you can go down two at a time, you and Gran, then Mum and Jack."

"What about Montgomery?" asked Jack.

"Oh, I don't think he will be interested in an old trunk, Jack," said Ben. So with torches and the key, Ben and Alex set off for the cellar.

Dorothy M. Mitchell

CHAPTER FIFTEEN
Treasure and Truth

The two men made their way along the tunnel, which
was becoming familiar to them now. They reached the
rock fall and Ben said, "Lucky we didn't shore up this
part of the wall, Alex. Strange how fate dictated that we
secure the cellar end first. It's more than strange, it's as
if something was telling us not to."
They came to the trunk and waited with baited breath.
Ben put the key into the lock of the trunk and turned it.
"That was quite easy Alex, the oil did the trick" The lid to
the trunk was lifted by the two very inquisitive men.
They pushed it wide open, then stood back amazed.
They were shining their torches on more brilliant jewels
and coins than either of them could ever have imagined.
Ben was the first to speak. "It's full to the brim! Who
would believe it? I just can't take all this in, there must
be thousands of pounds worth of treasure here. It's the
stuff you read about in adventure books but never in
your wildest dreams do you ever think it will happen to
you."
Alex motioned to Ben. "Look," he said. "There's
something written inside the lid." The two men shone
their torches on what looked like a piece of parchment,
and to Ben's utter astonishment, they read the words
that made both men gasp:

LET IT BE KNOWN THAT I, CAPT MATHIUS
BLACKTHORN OF THE SILVER MIST, BETTER
KNOWN AS BENJAMIN CHARLES BRISTOW,
ACQUIRED THIS BOOTY WHILST PRIVATEERING

ON THE SPANISH MAIN DURING THE YEARS OF
OUR LORD 1585 TO 1594

"Good grief!" exclaimed Ben. "This means my ancestor
was a pirate. I can't take this in - a pirate! What the heck
do we do now?"

"Hang on, Ben." Alex was remembering something. In
his capacity as a historian, he had read an article on
treasure troves. "This is a treasure trove. Come on, let's
go and tell the rest." So with great excitement all the
family crowded down the tunnel to take a look.

"This is like a dream," said Celia, running her hands
through the jewels. "Look at the rubies and sapphires.
Aren't they gorgeous? Who would think they had been
down here for all those years?"

"And the coins," said Jack, picking up a handful. "It
can't stay down here now, but it's too heavy to move."
Jess was getting in a bit of a panic. "I know how we can
move it; if we get the buckets and use them to take the
treasure up to the cellar, then we can get the trunk up
afterwards."

"Brilliant, Jack," said Ben, proud of this son of his, but
what nobody saw though was the young monkey take a
few coins out of the trunk and put them into his pocket.

"I will be the only boy at our school with treasure coins,"
Jack smiled to himself. This was all so exciting; no other
boy in the whole world was as lucky as he was.

Buckets were duly employed on the boy's suggestion
and they staggered positions along the tunnel in order to
pass the precious cargo to each other. Barnaby had
been called upon to help with the exciting job. He just
couldn't believe his eyes when they alighted on the
treasure. "Good heavens! It's been down here all these
years, and we knew nowt about it. It's amazing, just
amazing!"

It was decided that as the tunnel was too long for the snake of people to reach from the trunk to the cellar, they would work like this. Ben would fill the buckets one at a time, then pass each one to the next in line, who would pass it to the next, then move to the front of the snake, so creating a conveyor belt system, and after about three hours, all the buckets full of treasure were in the cellar.

"Now all we need to do is get the almost empty trunk up the tunnel, and into the cellar," said Ben, looking at his son. "My, but that was hard work, but it was a brilliant suggestion of yours, lad. It was the best way to do the job."

Celia spoke up. "I suggest we lock the tunnel door now."

"And before we go any further," said Alex, "we must inform the authorities."

Ben said, "I have been thinking; how about I get in touch with our solicitor in Axenby, Mr Julian Somers. He will advise us as to the best action to take."

"Good idea," said Jess. "We must do everything correctly and above board." And with that, and the tunnel door being well and truly locked, they went into the kitchen to be greeted by a very sorry for himself Montgomery, and Hetty, who gave a disdainful stare, as if to say, "Oh, you're back then?" and carried on washing her face and ears.

Ben walked over to the phone to inform Mr Julian Somers of the find, and arranged to see him shortly. Mr Somers arrived at the Grange with all the information needed. When he was taken into the cellar his eyes almost popped out of his head. "In all my days I have never witnessed such wealth," he said, looking at the buckets full of gold and silver coins and the most exquisite jewellery he had ever set eyes on. "Now, Mr Bristow," he said, "before we go any further, I must tell you that what you suspected is true. This is mostly treasure trove, and, my goodness, this is quite a haul. You must get in touch with the local police. They will inform the District Coroner, who will convene an inquest to decide whether all or part of the find is treasure trove. He has also to decide whether the material was hidden deliberately and not just lost, but I would imagine in this case that you being the finder and the landowner, it should be straight forward; however, I am not an expert in such matters, but first get in touch with the police. They will put you right."

Ben thanked the solicitor for all his advice, and the police duly arrived at the Grange; Inspector Phillips and two plain clothes officers. Ben took them to the cellar. "I'll bet you didn't expect this, Mr Bristow?" said the inspector. "This doesn't happen every day, and in all my years in the force, I've never seen anything like it."

"It's the last thing any of us expected," said Ben. "We came to Yorkshire to start a new life, but hidden treasure was the last thing any of us thought of."

After all the questions had been answered, the trunk was dragged outside, and the buckets of treasure were emptied very carefully, one at a time, back where they had been for hundreds of years. The trunk was then lifted by the three policemen, Ben and Alex taking up positions at intervals around the huge trunk, and with a lot of puffing, panting, and manoeuvring, the trunk was placed in the police van. One of the plain clothed policemen took his handkerchief from his pocket and mopped his brow. "By gum, that was heavy," he said.

"It's all that pudding tha missus gives thee, Frank," said the inspector, with smiles all round and a promise to keep in touch. The police turned the van towards the drive and drove away with the precious cargo.

CHAPTER SIXTEEN
Finders Keepers

With the trunk and treasure safely in good hands, life at the Grange took on a simpler, less hectic way of life. Spring was in the air; buds could be seen forming on the trees in the orchard; the sky was becoming quite blue, and the sun that had been in short supply for so long was getting quite warm. Barnaby could be seen going round the orchards cutting the grass with the old lawnmower, and at the same time, making mental notes of the jobs to be done in the gardens: branches up big trees which needed lopping. He told Ben that the winter had done a fair bit of damage, and Ben agreed with his gardener. "Just let me know when you are about to start and I'll give you a hand," he said.

Jess and Celia had started on the decor again, choosing fabrics and patterns for this room and that room, and Alex was a frequent visitor, spending more time at the Grange than his own home. The children were as happy as ever, Alice enjoying her pony lessons and wanting a pony of her own more and more; Jack on the other hand was in for a nasty surprise.

Jess had finished the laundry and was putting Jack's clean clothes away in his room when on opening his sock drawer, she found stuffed in the back three gold coins and two silver ones. "The little monkey," thought Jess, holding the coins in her hand. "When did he take them? It must have been when they were first discovered. Turn your back and if he feels like a bit of mischief, he just goes right ahead and does it."

Jess put the coins in her pocket, and when she had put Ben and Celia in the picture, it was decided that the lad must be taught a lesson. Jack arrived home from school and threw his satchel on to the chair in the kitchen. "Can I have a drink of pop, Mum?" he said.

Jess looked at her son, and, taking the coins from her pocket, held them out to the surprised boy. "Can you tell me anything about these?" Jack stood, not looking at his mother, his face crimson, he started shuffling his feet as if trying to think up some excuse.

"I only borrowed a few. They belong to us anyway," he said.

"But Jack, we don't know that yet. They are a very important find and that's why the police took them away. Now go to your room until we decide what to do about the situation."

Jack bowed his head and tried to hide the hot tears that started to run down his face. He loved his mum and she was cross with him. Ben decided the course of action to take was to get in touch with Inspector Phillips at the police station, after having a few words. Ben smiled when it was decided that he would take the boy along to the station. "It may just be enough to give the boy a scare," he said, so Ben and his son went to the station and walked up to the desk.

Inspector Phillips was waiting. "Now then, young fella me lad, what's all this?" he asked Jack.

Jack put his head down as the Inspector gave Ben a wink. He felt sorry for the lad, but he had to be taught a lesson, so after a good ticking off, Jack and his father left the police station. It had been decided that as all the booty in the trunk hadn't been catalogued yet, the five coins could be put back where they came from.

Young Jack was relieved to be going home, as it had been quite an ordeal for him, but he hadn't meant to steal the coins, he had just wanted to show his friends his real treasure. He was the only boy in the whole school who had some. With the ordeal over, Jack comforted himself that he hadn't been put in jail and he was going home to his mum. After a cuddle, and some of his mum's cottage pie, things started to look better. Jack and Montgomery stayed around the house, for it was half term and Mum had told him she didn't want him going far. Anyway the episode with the coins had given him quite a scare, so the lad did as he was asked and stayed around the house.

After a few days of messing about doing nothing in particular, Jack wandered into the big sitting room where they had discovered the key that had unlocked the treasure chest. Jack and Montgomery sat on the hearth of the huge fireplace pondering, for things had been pretty quiet and the young lad was feeling a bit fed up.

He sat wondering, how did the little boy chimney sweeps manage to climb all the way up those chimneys? He stood up and peered into the blackness of the chimney. "I'll bet they didn't have a torch," and with that Jack reached up, felt for one of the pegs that he knew was there, tugged at it, felt round for another, grabbed hold and pulled. He was off the ground, so he carried on feeling, and climbing. Montgomery, sensing his master was in trouble, started to bark. Up and up Jack climbed, and soot started to fall all over the hearth, carpet, and hapless dog. Then, "Dad, dad!" came down muffled cries.

Montgomery, now in a panic and almost covered in soot, ran towards the sitting room door as the family, hearing all the commotion, came rushing in. "Oh, no! Not Jack again, and just look at the carpets!" said Celia. With muted sounds coming from the chimney and a dog blinking his eyes trying to clear the soot which was by now trailed all over the carpets and furniture, Celia cried out in alarm, "Never mind the soot; what about Jack?" and there was a degree of panic. Everyone rushed to the fireplace crying, "We're here, Jack. Can you call out so that we can get your bearings?" Ben was shining his torch up the chimney, and a weak voice sort of croaked back, "I'm scared, Dad," followed by another cloud of soot billowing down covering Ben and the rest of the worried family. "I'm stuck, Dad, and I can't move."

"Hang on and we'll get you out. Jess, love, will you phone the fire station and ask them to come? Explain the situation," said Ben to his wife.

Jess set off and returned shortly, saying the fire fighters were on their way and to keep talking to Jack until they arrived. The fire engine pulled up outside the main door of the Grange, sirens telling of their arrival, and the crew came into the house: three fire men and one young woman fire fighter.

"We thought it best to bring Clare, our petite crew member, as she is very good at getting into difficult places, and judging by what you say," said the chief fire fighter, "she will be needed." Needed she was, for Clare called up the chimney saying, "Jack, can you call out so I can try to work out how far up you are?"

Jack gave a weak cry and Clare said, "OK love, try to keep still, and I'll be up in no time." With that, a sturdy rope was tied around Clare's waist and she started to climb, trying to reassure the frightened boy. Then after what seemed ages to Jack's worried family, the fire fighter emerged very sooty with a little black boy... well, black except where tears had run down his face, and left streaky pale marks.

Montgomery wagged his tail and proceeded to lick his master's sooty black face, while Jess with tears of relief laughed at the scene before her. "Oh, just look at the pair of them! I wish I had my camera handy, but I'll tell you one thing, you are not trailing all that soot into any of the bathrooms. I think the best place for you, Jack, is the large sink in the tack room, and will you please take Montgomery outside, Ben, and do your best with him in the old tin bath? I know he doesn't like a bath, but he will have to put up with it."

Celia spoke up now. "Don't worry about the carpets, I will soon have them as good as new," and everyone got on with the job in hand, and shortly things were back to normal, as normal as anything could be at Willerby Grange.

CHAPTER SEVENTEEN
Merlyn and the Goal Posts

Time went on apace, the soot incident forgotten, except when anybody mentioned the sooty boy, and it caused renewed laughter. It was well into spring, and the fruit blossom in the orchard was a picture. Celia sat with easel and canvas trying to recreate the beauty of nature with her paint brush: colours of delicate pinks and creamy white mingled with fresh new green shoots, apple and pear tree vying for prominence.

Celia sat back in her chair, and thought to herself, "This really is a picture that no artist could paint. God is the artist here and He can't be bettered." Alice came to where her grandmother was sitting. "That's good, Gran," she said, for Alice had always admired Celia's painting.

"Thank you love, that's kind of you. What are you doing? I thought you were going to Axenbey with your mum."

"No," Alice replied. "Since we came back from the stables I've just been messing about; anyway, Dad went with her."

Celia smiled to herself. So they had gone to do what they had discussed earlier. It was May, 1980, almost the girl's birthday, and this precious child could think of nothing else except owning a pony of her own. Secret preparation had been going on for some time. Barnaby and Ben had been hard at work making sure the old stables would make an adequate home for the newest member of the family's pets.

Alice had taken a shine to a young pony called Ned. She didn't like that name, because it was too old for such a lovely pure white colt, which always seemed happy to see her. His gentle eyes always spoke to her and she loved Merlyn. This had always been her special name for him, and she always sought him out on each visit to Blueberry stables; how she loved him!

"Well, Barnaby, I think the stables are ready," said Ben. "But how we have managed to keep our activities quiet I just don't know. Once or twice I thought Alice was going to discover our secret."

"Me an' all Mr Ben, but it's only a few days till the 20th. That's on Friday isn't it; afternoon, you say? Well, when the lass comes home from school she's in for quite a surprise. What a lovely birthday she's going to have. She's told me at length all about Merlyn, and me knowing that you and Mrs Jess had bought the colt for her birthday, well, I just don't know how I kept it to myself. OK, Mr Ben, now we've finished that job, I'll carry on with the goal posts for the lad. They've painted up quite well, an' when I've dug the holes to plant 'em, they should look all right."

"Give me the nod when you're ready, and I'll give you a hand," said Ben.

"Right you are, Mr Ben," said Barnaby, and when the posts were quite finished, the old gardener called on Ben. The two men carried and positioned the goal posts into the correct places, for they had previously measured the field to make sure the job would be done properly. "My goodness," said the exhausted gardener, "it looks like a proper football field now, though I say so myself."

"We've done a good job," said Ben, "and I think Jack will be very happy."

The day of the birthday arrived and Alice received many cards, together with one or two nice gifts from school friends; also a finely knitted scarf and gloves from Nora and Barnaby. However, the best gifts of all had been the jodhpurs from her mum and dad and the leather-riding boots from Gran. She had gone to school a very happy girl that morning, telling herself that one day she would get her best wish of all.

Mum and Gran had really gone to town with the birthday tea, with all the usual party stuff, sandwiches, jelly and ice cream, but the best of all was the birthday cake. It was made in the shape of a horse shoe, and while they were enjoying this excellent spread, Mum informed the party girl that a special lesson had been arranged at the stables, so why didn't Alice put on her new Jodhpurs and boots?

Alice complied happily, for it was a lovely birthday. "Come on then," said Ben. "We don't want to be late."

Alice was the first outside, heading for the car. Alice looked towards her dad to see the rest of the family going in the opposite direction from where the car was parked. Suddenly she had a strange feeling, for they were all going along the side of the house towards the back. Alice followed. She hadn't been along here for ages, so what was going on?

As the family reached the old paddock she heard a familiar sound. "It's my Merlyn!" she cried, and there in the smart new building was her beloved pony, looking over the stable door. Alice stood quite still and not a word was spoken as the family looked on. They saw tears of joy well up in the eyes of their precious girl, the girl who for so long had dreamed of this day.

Alice walked slowly over to the pony, gently putting her arms around her Merlyn. He gave a soft whinny and nuzzled his head into the arms of his mistress. He had come home, and Alice loved him. This lucky pony was going to spend the rest of his life at Bristow Grange.

Alice turned to her family, "Oh, Mum," she said and Jess put her arms around her daughter. "How can I thank you all? It's the best birthday ever."

"You can ride him round my football pitch, if you like," said Jack, who was quite happy that his sister had a pony. He liked the name Merlyn. It was a magic-sounding name. "Mind you," he added, "you can only ride around the outside, not near my goal posts."

Everyone laughed, for this had been the most happy of days. "Now, Alice, I expect you to take care of Merlyn in a very responsible way," said her dad. "It's your job to make certain that his stable is kept clean at all times, and that he gets adequate exercise."

"Oh Dad, of course I will, clean hay, and water every day," she replied.

"It's a huge responsibility for you," said Ben.

"Dad, I love him and I will love looking after him," said Alice.

So Jack had his football field, Alice her Merlyn and the result was two very happy children.

CHAPTER EIGHTEEN
The Thank You Gift and a June Wedding

"I've been thinking, love," said Ben, and Jess looked up from her writing towards Ben, who looked deep in thought.

"What is it, Ben?"
"You know when we all went to the fire station to thank them for all their help getting Jack down the chimney? Did you notice they didn't have a television in their rest room? What do you say we buy them a portable telly?"
Jess liked the idea; after all, Clare had probably saved Jack's life.
"And how about a couple of armchairs as well? They could certainly do with some," said Jess.
Ben agreed with Jess, who was once again showing her generous nature, and Mr Phillips seemed over the moon with the thank you gifts; and the family enjoyed the satisfaction of knowing that one good turn really does deserve another, so they were all pleased with the outcome.
As Ben, Jess and Celia sat in the kitchen enjoying a cup of tea, they were reflecting on the kindness of Barnaby, for he and Nora had been absolute angels ever since the Bristow family had moved into the Grange, and Barnaby's latest show of kindness was to make a set of low wooden jumps for Alice and Merlyn when they were on the field. The girl had been talking about a gymkhana friendly, between the Blueberry Stables and Lowforth Stables, in the next village. The family thought it an excellent idea, so arrangements were being made

for this pony show, and another important event was the marriage between Celia and Alex.

Of course, the joining of these two had been on the cards ever since that first meeting in that lovely restaurant in Exerby village, so when Alex had popped the question Celia had happily accepted. It had also been decided that the couple would make their home at Willerby Grange, so arrangements were being made for an apartment to be built by combining one of the sitting rooms at the back of the house with a newly constructed kitchen and bathroom. All had to be built to certain specification, for the Grange was a listed building, so with the wedding being planned and the apartment under construction, it was the usual pandemonium that the family had become accustomed to ever since moving to Yorkshire, but wasn't it exciting!

"We have decided to spend a few days in Whitby for our honeymoon," said Celia, rather shyly telling her daughter and son-in-law.

"Mum, that will be lovely," said Jess, giving her mum a big hug.

It was decided that the wedding day would be June 15th, and St Peters was to be where the happy couple tied the knot. The gymkhana was to be the following Saturday afternoon, and from then on until the day of the wedding, The Grange was a hive of activity.

Celia decided on a dress of pale oyster silk, hat and gloves to match, and Alice, who was the bridesmaid, was to wear a dress of the palest peach taffeta with shoes and gloves of a darker peach. The men, who included a reluctant Jack, were to wear peach bow ties. The lad reckoned it was better than being a page boy. He loved his gran very much, but a pageboy, Yuk! He wasn't going to be turned into a sissy.

St Peter's Church was decked out for the wedding and friends from the village had been happy to lend a hand, both at the Grange preparing for the big day, and putting flowers all around the inside of the church. On the aisle side of each pew was a sweet scented posy to line the bride's walk as she went to meet the man who was soon to be her husband.

The bride looked radiant, and Alice felt so happy, for she never thought in her wildest dreams that one day she would be bridesmaid to her lovely gran. So, Celia and Alex became Mr and Mrs Garside and the wedding was perfect. Family and guests arrived back at Willerby Grange for the buffet, and it was a beautiful day all round. Speeches were made, hearty thanks were given to all who had contributed to the happy day, and goodbyes were said as the happy newly weds left for a short honeymoon in Whitby.

Ben put his arm around Jess, saying, "You okay, love?"

Jess said, "Ben, didn't they look happy? Mum deserves all the happiness she can get, and I know that if my dad can see her, he will wish her all the best."

As Ben looked at his Jess, she started to cry, and he pulled her to him, saying, "I know, love. I know. Come on, let's have a nice cup of tea."

Whilst enjoying the wedding, Clare, the young lady fire-officer, overheard Jack telling young George Harper about his escapade up the chimney. "You know what boys are, Mr Bristow," she said. "Jack was going to great lengths as to how easy it had been, showing a bravado that seemed to be impressing his young friend. Whilst listening to their conversation, it struck me that he may just try the hazardous climb again to impress his audience, so I have a plan that will stop the little monkey in his tracks. I'll come round on Monday evening and cut the bottom few pegs with my bolt cutters."

"Good idea, Clare. That will stop his gallop," said Ben, and the helpful fire-fighter arrived on Monday evening as planned, and cut as many pegs as she could comfortably reach.

"Thank you so much," said a relieved Jess. "That's one worry off my mind." And the next time Jess saw Irene Harper she told her friend about the trauma of the chimney, as they sat in the little restaurant in Axenby enjoying a coffee together. They mused on the turn of events that had brought Irene's neighbour and Celia together.

"Alex deserves the best," said Irene. "We were quite concerned for him after his wife passed away, but the turn of events since you came to live in Yorkshire is the stuff dreams are made of. His house sold quite quickly, so we have new folks next door, a nice young couple with a baby girl. Are the honeymooners still in Whitby?"

"Yes," said Jess. "They come back next Saturday."

"That's the day of the gymkhana, isn't it?" said a very interested Irene. "Do you want any help?"

"Oh, Irene, could you? There is so much to do, and I really miss Mum, for she is a dab hand at organisation."

The friends parted company, looking forward to their next meeting on the day of the gymkhana. When the day arrived the sky was blue, with no hint of rain; people were busying themselves with setting us various stalls; horse boxes were arriving on the field; people were running shouting instructions; bales of hay could be seen scattered around; goods were being delivered to the various stalls and tack of every description was being set up; the loud hailers were being given an airing; in fact, it was hullabaloo, as ponies were being given exercise. And so it went on, until finally everything was ready for the gymkhana to begin.

Stirring music was played as Ben took to the stage and said, "Ladies and gentlemen, I would like to thank you all for coming to the first gymkhana to be held at the Grange. May it be the first of many more to come? So with no further ado, I declare the Bristow Grange gymkhana open."

The Mayor of Axenby took the stage and shouted, "Three hearty cheers for Mr Ben Bristow. May he and the family be very happy in their new home!" Then everyone clapped their welcome to the Bristow family.

"Gran! It's Gran and Alex," said Jack, the first to see his gran come on to the field, and it was a very happy Jess who threw her arms around her mum.

"You are both just in time to watch Alice and Merlyn do their turn," she said, flinging her arms around her mother and kissing Alex.

When the gymkhana came to an end, Alice and her beloved pony had won a first prize and a third, making for a very happy Alice and family. As the happy girl walked Merlyn to his stable, she felt so proud of her pony, placing the rosettes he had won over the stable door. Then she proceeded to give him a good brush down, after first removing his saddle. He was sweating rather, as the afternoon had turned rather warm, but after a while he appeared more comfortable. His stable had a quiet aspect, and he accepted a cool drink and settled down.

Alice gazed lovingly at this little pony who had just given of his best. He came towards his mistress and gently lowering his head and nuzzled her in the familiar way she had become used to - girl and pony in perfect harmony, while back at the Grange the rest of the family were enjoying a cup of tea together.

Celia and her new hubby looked very relaxed and happy. "Did you go for a paddle, Gran?" asked Jack.

"No, but we went for some lovely long walks along the cliffs, and we had a nice day trip to Bridlington, a lovely old world seaside town, but it's nice to be home." Celia looked at Alex; home, yes the Grange really was the best place ever, especially now that she and Alex were together as man and wife.

After a long chat and a light meal the newly weds retired to their apartment, for it had been a long day. Meanwhile Jack and his father were having a bit of a contretemps. "Jack, will you please stop messing about?" said his dad. "It will be too dark to do anything, and you did promise to help Barnaby put the jumps in the old barn. You can't very well expect to have a football match until they are put away."

"But Dad, it's not for a couple of weeks," pleaded Jack.

"I know all that, but you can't leave everything until the last minute. Now go on!"

So scuffing his feet, hands in pocket, Jack made his way to the bottom field. Barnaby waved him to come on and said he thought he'd got lost. "I've shifted most of 'em, and there's only these two left. Now come on and shape thyself. I want to get them all put away while we've still got a bit of daylight." The job done, man and boy made their way back to the Grange.

The day of the football match finally arrived and it was pouring down in torrents. "Well, would you believe it? Mid-July," said Ben, looking at Jess. "Do you think we should cancel?"

"I don't know, love," she answered. "There will be a lot of disappointed kids if we do. Let's see if the weather improves over the morning." By lunch time lady luck seemed to shine on the occasion, and the sun peeped out from behind the dark clouds, so by two pm the pre-season match between the village schools of Axenby and Lowforth was under way. Parents from both schools came along to cheer their respective team, with much cheering and clapping, the atmosphere was jovial, and the banter between parents of both sides was very friendly. Then came the deluge.

Without warning the skies opened, and in no time at all, players and spectators were soaking wet; however, what was to cause much laughter among the parents was the fact that both teams were determined to carry on playing in what had become a mud bath. It was impossible to tell who was who, as the players squelched and squirmed in their determination to carry on with the match, which finally ended two all. Luckily, Ben and Barnaby had erected a large tent earlier, fearing there may be summer storms, and how right they were. As people enjoyed refreshments provided by Celia and Jess, some were almost in hysterics at the thought of the muddiest football match they had ever witnessed, and the determination of the players not to give in. Jess offered a bath to any boy who would like to clean up; however, most declined.

But after everyone had gone home, Jess soon had young Jack in the tub, and she couldn't help smiling to herself at the muddy good day. Jack was singing to himself in the bath. Yes, on the whole it had been a good day, albeit a very wet one.

CHAPTER NINETEEN
Different Kinds of Treasure

A few days after the soggy football match, a letter arrived from the Coroner's Office informing the Bristow family that all the legal proceedings regarding the treasure found at Bristow Grange had been catalogued and dealt with. Museums around the country had shown enormous interest and had bought at current prices most of the find. The handful of precious stones not mounted on gold or silver would be returned to them, and the coroner took the unprecedented steps of allowing Jack to keep two of the coins, one gold and one silver.

The proceeds from the sale of the treasure were to be divided between the owner of the property where the treasure was found and equally between the finders. This meant one half to Ben and one quarter each to Alex and Barnaby. The amount of the reward came to a staggering one and a half million pounds.

When this good fortune finally sunk in, it was decided that they would give a generous portion to the local orphanage, also St Peter's Church for the restoration fund, and when all the excitement finally settled down and things started to get back to a semblance of normality, the family were sitting in the garden, on a lovely early August evening. "Do you know," said Celia, "I've been thinking. How about a garden party? We could invite the people of the village and make it something to remember."

"Mum, what a lovely idea," said Jess, getting into the swing of it. "Yes, let's have a really sumptuous do, fancy dress, pretty lights, music - the works, a party to remember.

Ben looked at Alex and they both smiled. "Here we go again." So once again the Grange was to be the venue for yet another extravaganza. The family members set to work, discussing this proposal and that proposal, for this was going to be the party that people would really enjoy, and talk about for a long time. It would take a great deal of organisation, but they all knew that anything enjoyable was not easily accomplished.

It was decided to hold the big day on August bank holiday Monday, and the first job was to send invitations to all the people of the village and surrounding area. It was also decided to erect a marquee and employ caterers. The Reverend Paul Jeffrey was roped in to help, and when Ben told him of the plan to have a bonfire on the beach as part of the festivities to bring the day to a close, incorporating a sing song, the vicar was delighted. "A sing song round the camp fire, that sounds lovely, Mr Bristow," he said. Invitations were sent out, and almost everyone sent back their acceptance.

The Grange was always at its best during functions involving happy events. It was as if the old girl relished being brought back to life. The sighing sounds had gone, the opening up of the secret tunnel had put paid to that; the sad haunting sound had gone forever, to be replaced by life and laughter. Before the great day the family attended church as usual, and St Peter's looked lovely decked out in autumn flowers. The congregation greeted the Bristow family with smiles and nods, and it was obvious they were looking forward to the party the next day.

The Reverend Jeffrey shook hands with Ben, and acknowledged the family, saying, "Nice to see you all again, and I am looking forward to tomorrow very much."

Monday arrived, the sun was shining, birds were singing and the Grange was like a lovely mad house. The marquee had been erected, caterers were feverishly working, and fairy lights were being placed around the gardens. But it had been decided not to include the fancy dress, because it would be inappropriate as it had been decided to include sport, both in the bottom field and the beach later in the afternoon.

The time was fast approaching two p.m., and Alex turned to Celia. "Well, love," he commented, "if we aren't ready now, it's too late."

Celia gazed into the eyes of her new hubby, saying, "Sweetheart, we have all worked hard for days, and I just know everything will be fine." Then she planted a kiss on the lips of this wonderful man.

"Come on, Gran, it's time to open the gates," a voice called. It was young Jack, eager to get the party started. Celia looked at her grandson as the lad ran on ahead towards the main gate which was just being opened by Barnaby. People started to arrive, and soon the whole place was buzzing with activity. The bottom field was soon full of people taking part in the various games, the sack race being the most popular with the boys, especially when mates fell over and ended up in a heap. Laughter and giggles resounded all over the field. Small prizes were awarded to the winners of each event, be it the three-legged race or the walking race which had Jess in fits of giggles, or the ladies' egg and spoon race which Nora Sykes won, much to the surprise of Nora herself.

The sports event came to a close and tea was served in the marquee. Ben stood on a chair, coughed loudly and said, "Ladies and gentlemen, girls and boys, if you would care to make your way to the house, we have a surprise for you." So with much anticipation, the guests followed their host and Ben led them to the cellar.

"You may have heard rumours of a secret tunnel, pirates' treasure hidden for hundreds of years. Well, dear friends, it's all true!" Ben then proceeded to relate the story of how one really stormy day back in January the children were playing in the cellar, when Hetty the cat, nosy as ever, had found a small hole in the wall behind an old chest. The hole was so small, not even the smallest child would be able to follow her, and both children started to panic. "On hearing the commotion I went to investigate, and it was very obvious to me and the ladies that the wall was a later addition to the rest of the house. By now, Hetty was becoming distressed judging by the constant meows that could be heard from the other side of the wall and Alice was getting very upset. She dotes on the very spoilt cat, and no matter how we tried to coax the daft thing back the way she went in, it was all to no avail. Myself, Alex and Barnaby decided to knock the wall down, and what a pantomime that turned out to be. We found a tunnel, a rock fall, and Jack was injured, but what an adventure! As you will see for yourselves, the tunnel goes right down to the beach, and can you imagine how we felt when a large trunk was discovered? To realise that my ancient ancestor and owner of the Grange had been a secret pirate and his fishing fleet in Hull harbour was a cover for his true identity. It's the sort of fantasy story you read about but never expect to happen."

And with that, Ben proceeded to lead the wondering party down the tunnel, made easier now as electric lights had been installed. Soon everyone was on the beach and the talk was of pirates and hidden treasure. The summer sun was just disappearing into the calm sea, and its halo of red and gold shimmered goodnight. Barnaby had gone before the party guests, and already the bonfire was crackling its welcome. Shouts of delight as yet another surprise was unveiled.

The Reverend Jeffrey asked everyone to be seated round the fire, and asked if everybody who had brought an instrument would gather to the right of him and accompany Alex and the group of singers in a rendition of favourite songs old and new. Everyone clapped and cheered as Alex stood up and walked to the front, and, of course, Alex was prepared for this as were the church players. It had all been arranged beforehand, for they had all rehearsed in secret for the occasion, and as the gathering of happy people sang, accompanied by the excellent music, the evening took on a magic all its own. People remarked how incredible it was that from the beach the tunnel couldn't be seen from any direction.

Later in the evening supper was served by the caterers who brought laden trays of sandwiches, sausage rolls, soup, tea or pop, and lovely chocolate gateaux, the latter being a favourite with the youngsters; so for a while, eating and talking took precedence. All of a sudden young Jack who was missing from the group could be heard shouting, "Dad, quick. Montgomery has found something. I think it's more treasure." The assembled group dashed towards the urgent voice and found Jack on his knees next to a very busy Montgomery digging for all he was worth in the soft sand up against the rock, but not getting anywhere, for as Montgomery removed sand, it just filled the hole again.

"Out of the way," said Ben to the dog, and himself got down on all fours and started to drag the sand out. While he did this, Montgomery, with a silly look on his face and ears forward and tail wagging furiously looked at Ben from time to time as if to say, "You're my hero." Eventually Ben found one, solitary bone and Montgomery was ecstatic. Ben patted the happy dog and said, "I guess that's your treasure, boy" and everyone cheered, and thanked Ben for the entertainment.

Then they all returned to the dying embers of the fire and the Reverend Jeffrey began to speak. "I think you will all agree that today has been a most excellent time. The Bristow family have gone to great lengths to make sure that this party was the success I think we can all agree that it has been, just that, a wonderful occasion, so can I ask you all to put your hands together for Ben and all the family?" Then everyone started to clap and cheer. The vicar was right, it had been a glorious day. The vicar raised his hand and asked, "Can we close this beautiful evening with Come, ye thankful people, come?"

Happy voices sung with gusto and when the verse, "All is safely gathered in" was sung, Jess took hold of Ben's hand. How true that was. Ben had come through a great deal of anguish to get to where he was now, and she had suffered with him, cried with him at times. The hurt had been unbearable, for it seemed the pain of others' lives had been sitting on Ben's shoulders for an eternity, but at last it was as if an awful cloud had lifted and the sun was shining bright and clear. The dross that had plagued them for too long had gone, and the Bristows of Bristow Grange were ready to take their rightful place at last. As for Celia and Alex, well, their joy was the treasure each had found in the other.

The party came to a very happy end and people made their way from the tunnel into the cellar and out of the Grange. As the family stood on the doorstep, waving goodbye to the last of their guests, Alice turned to her Gran and with a cuddle said, "I know I didn't want to come to Yorkshire. But Gran, I'm so glad we did, because it's the best place in the whole world!"

Celia Garside smiled. She totally agreed.

www.ingramcontent.com/pod-product-compliance
Lightning Source LLC
Chambersburg PA
CBHW030344030726
47499CB00003B/892